shoot a sitting duck

SHOOT A SITTING DUCK

BY DAVID ALEXANDER

RANDOM HOUSE · NEW YORK

For Mother
With Love

shoot a sitting duck

Christmas Eve is the loneliest night in the year on Broadway.

Bart Hardin, managing editor of the *Broadway Times,* had put the paper to bed early that night, not only because Christmas is a slow season in the worlds of the theatre and the racetrack, which were the sole interests of the sheet he edited, but also because he doubted that any reporter or printer on the staff would be sober enough to write a story or set a head within another hour.

Hardin, himself, had just consumed six ounces of Irish whiskey and a pound of sirloin steak in the Saddle and Whip Café, and as he walked out of the restaurant the strangely deserted reaches of Times Square at this hour of the evening were suddenly shocking.

Broadway blazed as bravely as ever but the effect was that of a great house lighted for a party at which no guests appeared. A few passers-by scurried over the wide streets, seeming furtive as they lowered their heads to breast the gusty north wind that swept through the empty, glowing canyon with a throaty animal sound. The denizens of this tawdry alley, Bart thought, crawl into

3

their private holes when other men concern themselves with the warm and simple pleasure of the greatest of the holidays.

Hardin headed south, with the knife slice of the wind at his back, in the direction of his bachelor flat above Bromberg's Flea Circus and Fun Arcade on Forty-second Street. In front of him a young couple, their faces bright with cold and excitement, walked arm in arm. "Darling," the young girl said, "isn't it all wonderful? It's like a great, big Christmas tree."

Sure, Hardin thought. A Christmas tree in the reception room of a bawdy house, only the customers are too busy elsewhere to admire it. All at once the hard, frenetic radiance of the Big Street was flecked with wind-driven snowflakes and the pretty girl's enthusiasm grew more shrill. "It's snowing!" she exclaimed. "It's going to be a white Christmas, darling!"

No, honey, Bart thought. Even Christmases aren't white on Broadway. They're tattletale-gray.

It was Christmas Eve, but all the shops were still open at this hour of the night and dark, worried little men in dazzling haberdashery peered through their glittering panes anxiously, hoping to find customers to relieve them of their holiday overstock. Broadway's merchants had made ludicrously grotesque attempts to display their wares in seasonal settings. In one shop window a papier-mâché fireplace and mantel had been erected and from it hung black net, fancily clocked, chorus-girl stockings that looked like props in the studio of a photographer of pornography. In another window was a crèche depicting

4

a stable in a place called Bethlehem and above the plastic dummy-figures of the Mother and the Child and the Wise Men and the Shepherds and the farm animals was a rainbow rack of neckties handpainted with designs of breasty mermaids.

On every corner stood a red Santa Claus suit inadequately stuffed with a boozy Bowery bum who licked chapped lips behind his yak-tail beard and clanged a dolorous bell to lure coins into a cardboard chimney piece that the welfare organization which employed him had discreetly padlocked.

Hardin lived on Broadway and he was used to being lonely in a crowd. He regarded the world he lived in with a cynical, detached fascination that was expressed in the slangy, ebullient columns of the paper he edited. He was fully aware of the hard facts of his own hard little world and he was resigned to them. He knew that Broadway "pals" with their vociferous protestations of affection were different from friends, that Broadway's preoccupation with sex in all its forms was far different from human love, that footlight histrionics were poor substitutes for real emotion, and the knowledge seldom troubled him. But tonight, somehow, it was different. The emptiness of the Big Street that had become his life seemed to reflect an emptiness inside himself as he walked toward his residence above the Fun Arcade, where young men in leather jackets fired small-bore guns at pipes and ducks, and oversized fleas performed incredible feats beneath magnifying lenses. The snow was falling faster now. Hardin watched the snowflakes swirl

5

insanely in the lighted void, loath to land finally after their dizzy flight, and he thought of himself, and he laughed aloud at the comparison. The young couple in front of him looked back over their shoulders curiously.

Hardin was walking slowly and he wondered why. His zip-lined trench coat was not an ample shield against the cold and the blade-edge of the wind. Then he knew the reason. He really had no place at all to go on Christmas Eve and he liked the nearness of the young couple just in front of him. He felt sure they were from out of town and they were just married and were spending a Christmas honeymoon in New York. He wondered what it would be like to experience again the quality of wonder at Broadway's clamorous excitements. Their nearness was a warmth in the bright, cold winter night. The young couple turned a corner suddenly and Hardin saw them enter a hotel that was both respectable and economical. He had almost reached the building where talented fleas performed to an overture of exploding target guns. Above that was the place he called home and he was alone.

He wondered what he would do with the night. Usually he gambled his nights away or sat at a small table watching half-nude girls do the bumps and grinds that were supposed to afford sexual stimulation to jaded customers, or he stood and drank double draughts of Irish whiskey at the Sligo Slasher's Bar across from Madison Square Garden. None of these amusements appealed to him tonight. There is nothing more depressing than an almost-empty cabaret or a bar where only chronic alcoholics stand like dedicated zealots drinking desperately. And that was what the Broadway sucker traps and barrooms would be like on Christmas Eve, he knew. He doubted if he could find a game in progress anywhere. Even Moe Selig, the loan shark and gambling czar of the Big Street, probably had a plump wife and a brood of children in some suburban home and would be decorating a Christmas tree. The thought of Selig placing an angel on the top branch of his tree made Hardin chuckle wryly.

Bart had reached the decaying brick building that housed Bromberg's Fun Arcade and his own apartment. He was surprised to note that the shooting gallery was fairly crowded. He supposed that firing guns at sitting ducks was as good a way as any for stray soldiers and sailors and the lost souls of Broadway to spend Christmas Eve.

Hardin entered the building and mounted the steps toward his flat on the third floor. On the second floor was the entrance to the Flea Circus. As Bart passed the door, a dumpy, moon-faced little man with a spit curl stuck his head out and called, "Wait up a minute, Mr. Editor! For a good tenant who pays his rent on the dot I got a Christmas present!"

It was Bromberg, proprietor of the amusement parlor and Hardin's landlord. Bromberg ducked inside again, returned with a fifth of liquor in a holly-decked wrapper. "Irishman's whiskey I've got for you," he said. "Merry Christmas."

Hardin took the bottle, grinned, said, "Merry Christmas. And best wishes to the fleas."

"You think you make a joke," Bromberg replied. "But I will tell them. My fleas have more sense than my tenants and my customers."

Hardin went up another flight of stairs to his apartment. The dim, old-fashioned living room was in even greater disarray than usual. Hardin's colored cleaning woman was recovering from an appendectomy and the soiled laundry and empties had been left to clutter the premises for two weeks.

He threw his wet trench coat on a chair, switched on more light and was about to open Bromberg's Christmas gift when the phone rang.

Used to answering the phone on his office desk, Bart said, "Hardin speaking."

A voice that was almost conscientiously unctuous resounded in the earpiece: "Ah, Hardin! I'm surprised and delighted to find you home at such an early hour. I rather expected you'd be playing Santa Claus to Broadway cardsharps on Christmas Eve."

It was the voice of Bart's employer, Maddox Slade, who owned the *Broadway Times* and angeled many of the productions his drama critic reviewed. Slade, an aging man with Social Register ambitions, had been the Broadway world's best-known bachelor until a few months before when he had finally married one of his numerous "protégées" of the theatre, an actress of small talent and abundant physical appeal named Arlene Lash.

Bart said, "There aren't enough people on Broadway

tonight for a game of two-handed stud. I ordered an early press run and fudge-boxed the late race results from the Coast because it's Christmas, even for horse players. Is something wrong?"

"No, no," Slade assured Hardin. "This isn't a business call, my boy. It's strictly social. I know it's rather spur-of-the-moment and all that, but Arlene and I thought you might be alone and could come up and have a holiday drink with us. Not a party. Just a quiet hour or so at home. I have to leave about eleven-thirty. I always attend Christmas Mass at the Church of the Theatre at midnight. It's sort of a tradition with me."

Bart hesitated. He had been to Slade's elaborate duplex in Gracie Square before, but it had always been a business matter that had taken him there. This was the first time he ever had been asked there for a social occasion, and, knowing Slade, he felt there was a reason behind the invitation.

Slade said, "Do come, boy. Arlene is very fond of you, you know."

Yeah, thought Bart, who had known Arlene before she became Mrs. Slade. She's very fond of me because I wear pants. It's hardly a distinction.

"Besides," Slade went on, "we'd like to have your opinion on a work of art Arlene has purchased."

Hardin's brow creased in puzzlement. "I'm afraid I'm not an art critic," he told Slade.

Slade chuckled. "I know the pictures you like best are the ones on playing cards," he answered. "But come up anyway."

Hardin said, "Well, thank you, sir. I'll be there as soon as I can change my shirt. It shouldn't take long to get there. There's not much traffic on the streets tonight."

Bart opened the bottle of Irish Bromberg had given him and poured a generous drink from it, taking it straight without a chaser. He didn't especially relish an evening *en famille* with his employer and his employer's wife. Arlene Lash was a woman just past her first bloom, about his own age, Hardin judged. There had never been anything between him and the woman except the sultry and provocative glances she accorded every man she met as casually as she acknowledged an introduction. But sultry, provocative glances might prove embarrassing when her husband was present, especially since her husband was Bart's employer. Bart swallowed more whiskey, grinned as he thought, I guess maybe I'm too old for her even if we're both in our early thirties. When Arlene had been Slade's protégée instead of his wife, she had played patroness to a long series of young actors who were distinguished more by their muscularity than their dramatic genius.

Hardin found an unopened package of laundry on a chair and changed to a clean white shirt. As an afterthought he discarded the rather gaudy floral vest he had been wearing in favor of a charcoal number decorated by small embroidered rosebuds. Fancy vests were Hardin's trademark on the Big Street and this was the most conservative number that he owned. Even that will shock the doorman at Slade's ritzy pad, he thought.

In front of the Flea Circus he found a cab immediately. The driver gave him a big smile, said, "Good evening, sir, and Merry Christmas." When New York hack drivers get that polite, Bart thought, business is really lousy. The almost deserted, snow-swept streets were downright eerie. For once New Yorkers had remembered they had a home.

As the cab headed uptown on a street with staggered lights, the driver said, "It's a ghost town tonight. They had all the office parties yesterday and the drunks are either dead or safe at home by now."

The short extension of East Eighty-fourth Street called Gracie Square, which begins at East End Avenue and ends abruptly at the river, represents more massed money than any other 200 yards in the world. The owners of the money live in half a dozen massive, feudal towers that are huddled as close together as tenements in New York's lower slums. The rich men's front yard is Carl Schurz Park where grubby young urchins from the Yorkville section howl at their play. Directly to the east the dark, sluggish river makes a curve and most of the boats that ply it are not galleons bearing gold but scows redolent of the city's garbage. Across the little park is ancient Gracie Mansion where Washington once made his headquarters and New York's mayors make brief residence today. Across the river on Long Island are rows of barrackslike apartments from which shipping clerks and insurance salesman have as fine a view of the garbage scows as the millionaires who inhabit the Square's massive towers.

In deference to the doorman's tender sensibilities Hardin kept his trench coat buttoned over his floral weskit

11

as he entered the building. He could not conceal the decorative garment from Slade's man, Hodgson, who took his coat in the foyer. Hodgson had served Slade long before his employer's marriage. Sometimes Hardin suspected that Slade paid Hodgson more for shining his shoes and pressing his pants than he paid the editor of his newspaper.

Hodgson ushered Bart into the enormous living room of the duplex. Hardin had never seen this room before. On previous visits he had always gone directly to Slade's study, where all business was transacted. The study was a warm and cheerful room. Slade fancied himself an art collector and the study's walls were filled with fine Aiken racing scenes and amusing oils of the early London prize ring by Cobbett. This was a very different room indeed. Perhaps it expressed another facet of Slade's devious personality. It was cold, austere, and almost chastely classic. The carpeting was a purplish wine color, the walls and draperies gray, the furniture forbiddingly dark. Here the pictures on the wall were varnished, monotonic portraits by lesser masters of the Dutch school, the figures as stiff as the atmosphere of the room. There was one jarring note. A large canvas, unframed, was sitting on the mantelpiece. Even to Bart's untrained eye it was a horrible and amateurish example of modern abstract painting. In color it blended well enough with the room. It was heavily painted so that the direction of the brushwork was quite obvious, especially since there was a jagged unpainted border at the right where the careless artist had failed to complete his line of color. It was done mostly in blacks and tones of gray. But it definitely did not belong. It would be difficult to find a room in which it did belong, Bart thought.

Arlene, Slade's wife, was sprawled out in a chair. Her blue hostess gown fit her just a bit too snugly, as all her clothes did. The garment was obviously expensive but it was slightly rumpled. The shoulder-length coiffure of her bronze hair was obviously expensive, too, and it was also slightly rumpled. She'll be fat in a few years, Bart thought. But right now her figure's just interestingly female. Arlene's full lips were parted and her eyes were glazed and sulky. Bart suspected she had been drinking heavily. Before she had come under Slade's protection, Arlene had encountered trouble in the theatre because of her drinking. There was a cocktail glass in her hand and she waved it casually at Hardin in greeting.

Hardin had always considered Slade a caricature of the middle-aged man of distinction. Slade's face was baby-bottom pink, his hair was white and his heavy eyebrows jet-black. Bart had known skid-row bums and Jacobs Beach fight managers who had white hair and black eyebrows, but somehow this accidental pigmentation was associated in the public mind with men of achievement and social stature. Bart's host was impeccably attired in dinner jacket, black tie and cummerbund.

Slade advanced toward Bart, extending a manicured hand, and his heartiness was almost overwhelming. "Merry, merry Christmas!" he exclaimed. "So glad you could come, boy. Christmas Eve is a sentimental time when old friends are always best. I trust you got the little bonus and it was acceptable?"

Bart said, "Money's nice, but I always seem to find a place to blow it. This time it was a goat in the second at Florida."

Slade shook his head and chuckled patronizingly. "You should know better, boy," he said. "In your job you should know all gamblers die broke. You see it happen every day."

When Hardin was seated, Slade frowned at his wife and said, "You'll pardon if Arlene seems a bit on the sulky side, Hardin. She's bored and I hope you can cheer her up and make her show the proper Christmas spirit. It's partly my fault, though. We've had a little spat, a disagreement. I feel Arlene has been badly put upon. It's all about that monstrosity up there on the mantelpiece."

Slade waved a hand toward the black and gray abstract composition. Hardin looked at the painting, said nothing.

"But before we go into that," Slade said, "you must let me pour you a glass of this fine wine. . . ."

"Wine, hell," Arlene interrupted him inelegantly. "Hardin doesn't want that soda pop. He takes a man's drink. Irish. I had Hodgson bring a bottle in."

She slopped whiskey into an old-fashioned glass, spilling part of it on the handsome rug. She plopped an ice cube into the glass with her fingers, disregarding the silver tongs, and handed the glass to Hardin.

Slade's indignation was foolishly like that of a small,

disappointed boy. He said, "This soda pop happens to be a truly great year of Château Yquem I've saved especially for Christmas. And Arlene sits there drinking gin!"

Hardin said, "Sorry. I'm a lowbrow. Irish is what I like."

Arlene gave a short contemptuous laugh. "Maddox doesn't really drink," she declared, regarding her husband with open contempt. "He sips. He just sips at everything. Liquor and life were made to be gulped so you can get your kicks out of them."

It was a hell of a Christmas Eve, Hardin thought. Maybe it might be a fine rule never to answer telephones.

Slade said, "I want you to take a look at that painting, Hardin." He held up his hand as Bart started to protest. "Now, now, I know you're no connoisseur, but I want you to take a look at it and see if it says anything at all to you, if you discern the slightest bit of merit in it. But first I'll tell you about our little disagreement. Arlene is difficult to please. So instead of a present I gave her cash for Christmas. It's vulgar to mention this, of course, but I'm sure you'll understand. I gave her five thousand dollars. I expected she might buy a fur or a gem or perhaps a foreign sports car. Instead she bought that atrocious hunk of pigment that could have been purchased off a Greenwich Village fence at the outdoor show for fifty dollars at the most. I say she allowed pity for the artist to outweigh her judgment and she should get her money back."

Arlene's eyes were blazing murderously as she looked at her husband. Then she looked at Bart and the provocative expression he had seen before came into them. She said, "You know why you're here, Hardin? You think it's because you're an old friend and this is what Maddox calls a sentimental occasion? Well, that's not it. You're here because you're Maddox's hired hand and he needs a strong boy. You're an ex-captain in the Marines or something and you got your nose broken boxing once and you look tough. Maddox wants you to go down and browbeat a poor little artist in the Village so he can get his money back. Why should he hire a mobster when he's already got a managing editor?"

Slade's pink face flushed crimson. "That's outrageous!" he declared. "And of course it's completely untrue. Arlene has been victimized and she hates to admit it, so she's angry. She's been fancying herself as a patron of the arts, I believe. She has taken up with a group of artists and actors that centers around that little theatre movement—Opportunity, Incorporated, it's called, down on Bleecker Street in the Village. One of the members is this Erik Drake, whose name appears in a large scrawl over that abortion on the mantelpiece. Those grafting bohemians know she is well off and they've sold her a bill of goods after all her kindnesses to them. I won't tolerate it!"

Slade rose, took hold of Hardin's arm, urged him to his feet. He said, "Come over here, Hardin. Take a look at this thing and tell me what *you* think it's worth."

"This is silly," Hardin answered. "Bathing-beauty calendars are more my line."

Hardin looked at the picture closely. Against the dark background light gray triangular designs were arranged

16

in serried rows. Hardin said, "What's it supposed to be?"

"The title of it is 'Ducks Flying South,'" Slade replied.

Bart noted that the painting was leaning against the east wall of the room and that the easily discernible brushwork swept to the right and the apex of each of the small triangular designs pointed in the same direction.

He said, "Well, since the background's black, I guess it's night. If these little triangles are the ducks, they're heading to the right, which would be south, the way the picture's placed. So the ducks are heading in the right direction, even though it's pitch-dark. Smart ducks."

They were interrupted by the entrance of Hodgson into the room. He was bearing a silver tray with an envelope on it. The envelope was square and large like those which contain Christmas cards. It was of cheap, sleazy paper, Bart noted, like the envelopes of dime-store stationery. The very proper Hodgson handled it disdainfully.

The servant said to Slade, "Excuse me, sir, but the elevator boy just brought this up. It arrived by special delivery, I believe."

Slade took the card, appeared astonished. "Why it's addressed in pencil and it's printed!" he exclaimed. Slade thought it vulgar to send Christmas cards by special delivery at the last moment. His friends did not address their cards in pencil. And most of the cards he received were engraved by Tiffany.

Slade tore the envelope open, took out a card that pictured a large and florid Santa Claus. He opened the folder and as he read whatever was written inside, his face first took on an expression of dumb amazement and then he

17

broke into uncontrollable laughter. Bart had never seen his suave employer so perilously close to hysteria.

Slade thrust the card toward Hardin, his laughter still bellowing. "Read it, boy," he gasped. "You're mentioned in it."

Bart looked briefly at the rosy Santa Claus. Inside there was printed the usual message about a Merry Christmas and a Happy New Year. But the rest of the folder was covered almost entirely by a curious, slanted penciled printing.

MADDOX SLADE:

WE GOT YOUR WIFE. GET $50,000 IN $20 BILLS AS SOON AS BANK OPENS OR WE KILL HER. YOUR BOY HARDIN WILL BE GO-BETWEEN. TELL HIM TO STAY HOME AND WAIT FOR CALL ABOUT PAYING MONEY. HE WILL HEAR FROM US.

When Hardin had read the message over twice, Slade took it from him and handed it to his wife. He said, "Read this, my dear. Then tell me truthfully, Have you been kidnapped?"

Arlene took the Santa Claus card grudgingly, her face contemptuous. She read the printed message and her expression changed.

She's an actress, Bart thought, but she's not a very good one, and it's a dead cinch she's not acting now.

Her heavy makeup could not conceal her sudden, death-white pallor. Raw terror was written on her face.

Slade looked at his wife solicitously. "My dear!" he exclaimed. "What on earth's the matter? You look quite ill. It's only a joke you know, a very bad joke indeed, but still a puerile jest. Why should it have this effect on you?"

Rage had replaced the expression of fear on Arlene's face. She hurled the Christmas card at Slade. Her long red nails bit into her hands as she pounded the table with her fists, sending the martini shaker to the floor. Slade ducked to pick up the shaker before all its contents spilled over the purple rug.

"Who did this to me?" Arlene screamed. "Who did this filthy, rotten thing?"

Slade said, "I can only guess that it was your artistic friends in Greenwich Village. It seems fairly typical of their perverted sense of humor to inform a man whose wife is in his presence that she has been kidnapped and to write a ransom note on a Christmas card."

In an obvious effort to distract attention from his hysterical wife, Slade picked up the Christmas card from the floor. It was slightly dampened by the spilled martini. He dried it off with a linen handkerchief and handed it to Bart.

He said to his wife, soothingly, "You know, my dear, we're very lucky to have Bart Hardin here this evening. He's quite a detective. He's been mixed up in a couple of murder cases. Now, Hardin, you look at that card and tell us what you make of it."

Hardin took the card but did not look at it. He said, "I'm hardly a detective, but there was one thing I noticed when I looked at it. It was probably printed by a left-handed person. I'm no authority on questioned documents, either. But it just happens that old Pops Taylor, the turf editor at the *Broadway Times,* is left-handed and he always prints the heads he writes. His copy comes over my desk, of course. His printed heads have the same peculiar slant as this."

"Now, now, Hardin," Slade said, his manner offensively patronizing, "old Pops has worked for the paper nearly forty years. He was there long before I bought the *Broadway Times* back in the thirties. You're not telling me Pops would play a stupid practical joke like this, are you?"

"No," Hardin answered. "This printing is very different in the form of its letters, the way they're made. But the slant's the same. So maybe the writer is left-handed, like Pops."

"Are any of your Greenwich Village friends left-handed, darling?" Slade asked Arlene. He chuckled. "The Case of the Left-Handed Bohemian," he said. "A fine title for a whodunit, isn't it?"

Arlene was silent and glaze-eyed again and she seemed very drunk. Bart had noted that she was one of those women who have to have a large handbag beside her at all times. The handbag beside her on the chair was leather and did not complement her hostess gown. She opened the bag and her nervous hands fluttered inside it. A lipstick rolled to Bart's feet as it fell out of the bag, and it was followed by several cards and scraps of paper. Arlene finally found the pack of cigarettes she was looking for. Bart picked up the litter she had strewn over the floor, returning it to her. She stuffed it carelessly in her bag.

Slade had poured another glass of the Château Yquem from an ornate decanter of Belgian glass. His face was sober. He said, "Seriously, I do not regard this matter too lightly. I do not relish acting the role of the stern, unbending husband, Arlene, but I feel it is time I must forbid you to see any members of this Greenwich Village group again. They have taken the most outrageous advantage of you. I realize you are interested in young people in the arts, but this is going too far. They have not only cheated you out of a considerable sum of money, but they have seen fit to ridicule us both through this stupid practical joke."

Arlene's body stiffened and she glared at her husband.

Bart said, "You're quite sure the note is from one of her Village friends, aren't you?"

Slade nodded. "It has to be. They are the only people she sees outside of our mutual acquaintances and I assure you none of my friends could be guilty of such execrable taste. Frankly, Hardin, I intend to take action. Arlene was half-right a few minutes ago when she said I might try to enlist your help. Of course, the idea that I want you to act as a strong-arm man is completely absurd. I would appreciate your acting as a friend and emissary. It should be handled through an attorney, I suppose, but I hesitate to embarrass Arlene by letting Marty Land know how gullible she is. Marty is a Broadway lawyer and the story would be all over the Street and in the columns in no time at all. I would be very grateful if you would consent to see this Drake and tell him I will take legal action unless he returns the money. You can even offer him a small sum for taking the painting back and returning the purchase price. Men like him come cheap."

Arlene had risen to her feet. She stood over her husband and screamed at him. "I hate you! I loathe the sight of you, you hear?"

She ran across the big room and her high heels clattered on the circular stairway that led to the second floor of the apartment.

Slade's pink face had gone pale. He looked at Bart helplessly, shrugged. "The artistic temperament," he said. "You and I have been around theatre people long enough to be used to that, haven't we?"

Arlene was descending the stairs as hastily as she had mounted them. A fur coat was slung carelessly over the hostess gown and a filmy scarf was wrapped around her bronze hair.

Slade rose and said to her, "Where on earth are you going, Arlene?"

She called over her shoulder to him, "Out! Anywhere!"

"But, Arlene, we have a guest and it's Christmas Eve!" Slade protested.

Arlene was at the door to the hall of the duplex. She turned and faced her husband. "I'm sick of the sight of you!" she flared. "Can't you understand that? You're old! Old! Do you hear me? You're old!"

She ran out of the apartment. The outer door slammed after her.

Slade sank down into his chair and he suddenly became an old man in front of Bart's eyes. Hardin had always regarded his employer as a pretentious man of little sincerity. Now he felt deep pity for him. Looking at Slade, Bart thought of an old Marine commander he had seen in Korea on the night they learned the retreat route from the Yalu had been cut by the Chinese.

Bart averted his eyes, looked down at the floor. There was a scrap of paper on the floor at his feet. It must have dropped from Arlene's handbag with the other things while her frantic fingers were seeking the pack of cigarettes. He saw that there was scrawled, feminine writing on the paper. "Bromberg's Fun Arcade midnight." Bart's eyes narrowed. He thought of picking it up surreptitiously and stuffing it in his pocket. He considered handing it to

23

Slade. He decided to do nothing at all about it. He did not want to become involved in this. Just leave it to chance, he told himself. Maybe Slade will find it. Maybe a vacuum cleaner will suck it up.

Slade turned toward Bart appealingly. He said, "You understand she is intoxicated, Hardin. She had trouble with alcohol in the theatre. She had a hard time when she first came here as a young girl trying to break in, and she started drinking too much. I thought marriage and the little luxuries I could give her would solve the problem, but it hasn't worked out. She's not herself, Hardin."

Bart said nothing. Slade's eyes implored him. "Go after her for me. See she doesn't come to any harm," he said.

Bart rose. He said, "I'll go, but I doubt I can catch her now."

As Hodgson assisted Bart with his coat his controlled servant's face was impassive, yet somehow he managed to convey his amused gloating at the domestic scene which had just been enacted in the living room of the duplex.

On the street floor of the apartment house, Hardin approached the doorman and said, "Did you see which way Mrs. Slade went?"

The doorman's face was not as well controlled as Hodgson's. He smirked openly. His insinuating voice was downright insulting as he said, "She's waiting for you, sir, in a cab parked just the other side of the entrance to the building."

Bart stepped into the street, saw the yellow cab at the curbing in the direction of East End Avenue. Arlene leaned out of the taxi and beckoned to him urgently.

24

When Bart reached the cab, she said, "Get in, Hardin! Quick!"

Bart shrugged. Oh, well, he thought, I'm only following the boss's orders.

Arlene said to the driver, "Turn left at the corner and take East River Drive downtown at Seventy-ninth."

After they had driven onto the express highway, she turned to Bart, her face both drunken and frightened. She said, "I'm scared, Hardin. I'm scared to death. I'm in trouble. Bad trouble."

Bart said, "I'm sorry."

As they sped down the Drive, the cabbie looked back, asked, "Where you want me to get off the drive, madam? I've got to be in the right lane for the exit."

Arlene said, "Somewhere in the Forties. We're going to that Flea Circus on Forty-second Street."

Bart scanned his companion's face appraisingly. "I didn't know you were a patron of Bromberg's Flea Circus," he said.

Arlene's answer was short, emphatic. "We're going to your apartment, Hardin. I've got to have your help. I've got to talk to you."

Hardin said, "I don't think that's a good idea. The place is in a mess because the cleaning woman's been sick. Let's go somewhere and have a drink."

Arlene shook her head. "No. We're too well-known. Someone would see us and there'd be gossip and it would get back to Maddox. Things are bad enough already."

Hardin didn't argue further. After all, his employer had given him an assignment. The apartment would be as

25

convenient a place as any for watching over the intoxicated Arlene, he supposed. He did not look forward to spending Christmas Eve as the male nurse of a female drunk, however.

Arlene sat tense and silent for the rest of the drive, smoking one cigarette after another. When they reached the old brick building on Forty-second, she raced up the stairs ahead of Bart, averting her head as she passed the floors that housed the Fun Arcade and Flea Circus. Hardin let her into the flat, switched on lights, made rather futile gestures at cleaning up the worst of the litter.

Arlene said, "For God's sake pour me a drink."

"I haven't got a drop of gin," Bart told her. "All I drink is Irish."

"It's got alcohol in it," she replied. "That's all that matters."

Bart poured her a drink and she gulped it before he could offer water. She held out the glass for more. Hardin looked at her dubiously, poured half an inch of liquor into the glass. He said, "Pour some water in that one. And sip it, even if you don't like to sip."

Arlene took off her coat and scarf, sat down with the glass in her hand. She said, "I *had* to buy that painting, Hardin."

"Sure," Bart answered indulgently. "I hear all art collectors are fanatics. All I collect are bad debts and fancy vests."

"Nuts, Hardin. Don't treat me like a child. I'm not an art collector. I had to buy that painting so I could give Erik Drake five thousand dollars."

26

"That was very generous of you," Hardin commented.

Arlene said, "I'm not generous. I'm a selfish bitch, in fact. And I'm always in trouble because of young men and hard liquor, it seems."

"Was this artist Drake one of the young men?" Bart asked.

"God, no. He's not my type. A puny, frustrated, awful little man with a persecution complex. He has pimples on his neck and he bites his fingernails. He's a diry little blackmailer, Hardin. That's why I had to buy the picture."

She forgot to sip. She took the liquor at a gulp again, lit a cigarette off the butt of one that she was smoking. Hardin waited.

Arlene said, "Up to just a little while ago this Drake had a studio in the Village—it was a cold-water flat, really —with a young actor named Howard Barnaby. I—I was interested in Barnaby. He's just a baby, really. Twenty-three or twenty-four, I guess. A baby with the body of a heavyweight champion. I tried to help Howard. I got him readings with some of the best Broadway producers, Saul Josephs, Ben Lane Price, all of the big ones, but I couldn't sell the boy. He acts for nothing at that Opportunity, Incorporated Theatre down in the Village that is supposed to give young actors a break. He lives on a measly allowance from his father who has a little business somewhere out in Indiana. I would have helped him financially myself if I could have done so. I—I'm interested in the boy and I have faith in his talent. But Maddox just doesn't give me any money. Not cash. I've got accounts at the best stores and he gives me lavish presents, but my allowance

27

is less than that of the average housewife in the Bronx. And I have to account for every cent of that to him."

She thrust out her glass, said, "I need one, Hardin."

Hardin hesitated. "Take it easy," he warned.

Arlene flushed angrily, got up from the chair, grabbed the bottle Bromberg had given Bart. She said, "For God's sake, Hardin, quit acting like the mother superior of the W.C.T.U. I'm no tender vessel. I play all the games the boys play."

She filled the glass half full of Irish, disregarded the water pitcher, sat down again, placing the bottle conveniently at her feet.

Bart thought, Maybe it's better this way. He knew Arlene's drinking pattern. If she kept up like this she would pass out cold. That would solve the problem for a little while at least.

She drank from the glass and her words were more slurred when she spoke again.

"I went to see Howard at this studio he shared with Drake. Sometimes Drake was there. Sometimes he wasn't. A few weeks ago Howard had a fight with Drake and moved out. Then Drake started trying to blackmail me. He had a recording machine and he claims he left it open when Howard and I were there together and has transcripts of the things we said. He got hold of some foolish letters I wrote to Howard. He threatened to turn the records and the letters over to Maddox unless I paid him five thousand in cash. The Christmas present Maddox gave me was a godsend, but I had to have some way of explaining how I spent it. So I paid Drake five thousand for that horrible picture that's supposed to be flying ducks or something. Nobody else would have given him a subway token for that or anything else he's ever painted. I thought that would finish it, but it didn't. He demanded more, right away. I arranged to meet him tonight in this shooting gallery downstairs, in fact, to try and stop him. At midnight, because Maddox always goes to Midnight Mass on Christmas Eve." Bart thought of the scrap of paper that had fallen from Arlene's bag. He decided not to mention it.

"If this Howard Barnaby is such a big, strong boy, why can't he put the fear of God into a puny little guy like Drake?" Bart asked.

Arlene drank the rest of her Irish, poured more. She said, "I wouldn't dare tell Howard. He's just a baby. He couldn't cope with a thing like this. And he's got an awful temper. There's no telling what he might do to Drake if he knew."

Bart said, "You want me to go down and talk to Drake, is that it?"

Arlene was taking the shots of whiskey fast now. She gave Bart a searching glance and the warm, challenging look came into her face. Oh, oh, Bart thought. It's coming now. When Arlene drank, she was likely to grow amorous and it didn't take a twenty-three-year-old boy with a heavyweight's body to attract her.

Her voice was husky and the slurred words were drawled. "Would you do that for me, Hardin?" she asked. "You're a most impressive man, you know. You're attractive, too."

Hardin felt the need to divert the conversation from his dubious charms. He said, "Are you planning to keep the appointment with Drake downstairs in the Fun Arcade?"

Arlene shook her bronze hair. "Uh-uh," she said. "I'm afraid to, now. I've been afraid ever since that silly Christmas card arrived."

"You think Drake will try to kidnap you?"

"No. Of course not. But it's his dirty, nasty way of warning me that he means business and I'd better come with money, sending that card to Maddox at a time he knew I'd almost surely be at home because it's Christmas Eve. He's a twisted little man with a twisted sense of humor. That card was meant as a warning to me that he will stop at nothing and that he wants fifty thousand dollars before he's through. I can't get fifty thousand dollars. I'll have to let him do his worst."

She reached for the bottle and this time Hardin made no effort to stop her. Maybe he could figure some angle while she slept if she would only pass herself out. "Drink hearty," Hardin said. "You might as well be tight as the way you are now."

During the next twenty minutes Hardin's own eyes widened as he watched the liquor-line of the Irish bottle recede. During that time Arlene's conversation was desultory at best and toward the end it was completely incoherent. Finally her head sprawled back and her eyes closed. Breath wheezed out of her open mouth. The glamorous Broadway actress wasn't very glamorous at the moment, Hardin thought.

He had decided on a course of action. He was avoiding the issue, running away. But it was the best device he could think of under the circumstances. Arlene would be safe enough if he simply left her there asleep. When she awakened, she would doubtless be outraged at him for deserting her and would leave the flat. Hardin hoped she would go home because there was no place else to go. Leaving her like that might involve embarrassing explanations to Slade later. But the explanations wouldn't be as ridiculously embarrassing as resisting the intoxicated advances of his employer's wife if she awakened and he was still around.

Hardin got his coat and hat and tiptoed across the room, closing the door silently behind him. First, though, he hid the bottle and all the other liquor in the room. He went to the Sligo Slasher's Bar on Jacobs Beach, across from Madison Square Garden. Tony Maclaren who called himself the Sligo Slasher was a little bantam rooster of a man who claimed, without benefit of record books, to have been the lightweight champion of Ireland in a distant day. He was doing his best to entertain four drunk and despondent customers who were draped over his bar. Bart knew only one of the customers, a jerky, pathetic little man called Twitchy whose proudest boast was that he had been one of Dempsey's seconds in the Billy Miske fight.

Maclaren was saying, "In the Emerald Isle we always had championship bouts on Christmas Eve and they lit the great arenas with thousands of Christmas candles. When I was fighting Cleaver Carney back in 1923 the auditorium caught fire from the candles and the roof burned right off the place but the fight was so fine and fierce that not a single customer left. I knocked me opponent out just as the ringposts took fire and the referee's shirttails were blazing while he counted ten."

"You were just like old Jack," said Twitchy, nodding gravely. "You know what I could do right now? I could walk up to old Jack and say 'Merry Christmas' and you think he'd hand me a fin or a sawbuck or a C-note even? No, sir. He'd hand me a grand, that's what he'd do. Old Jack remembers what I did for him in the Miske go."

Bart drank his Irish slowly. He thought he could predict Arlene's behavior pattern from previous observation. She would sleep for only half an hour or so, he felt reasonably sure. He exchanged banter with Maclaren for the better part of an hour, then dropped a coin in the telephone and dialed the number of his flat. There was no answer. At eleven-thirty he wished Maclaren and his customers a Merry Christmas and walked to the door. Twitchy called after him, "Hey, Editor! You ever wanna meet Jack Dempsey, you come to me. Old Jack will shake the hand of a friend of Twitchy's any time."

It was still snowing as Bart walked down Eighth Avenue toward the Flea Circus. He passed a cheap picture house which advertised THE SHAME OF YOUTH, A DOCUMENTARY OF TEEN-AGE SIN AND SEX. ADULTS ONLY. Bart wondered what kind of adults attended sex films on Christmas Eve.

He glanced into the Fun Arcade as he entered the old brick building, wondering if Arlene had changed her mind about keeping the appointment with her blackmailer. He didn't see Arlene but he saw someone else, and he ducked back against the wall and hurried up the stairs. Maddox Slade was standing in a corner of the shooting gallery, his hat brim turned down, his coat collar pulled up, trying to make himself inconspicuous.

The lights were still on in Bart's apartment, but Arlene had departed. Before Bart could even remove his coat, the telephone rang. Bart hesitated. It would probably be Arlene, he thought, and that would mean further complications. Finally he picked up the receiver to still the clamorous clanging. He said, "Hardin speaking."

A man's voice, husky and obviously disguised, said, "Hardin, you shouldn't go out. We been calling. What time is it by your watch?"

Bart's brow creased. He glanced at his wrist watch, said, "It's eleven-forty-six, but you should call Meridian 7-1212 to get the correct time. It's a special service of the phone company."

The monotonic voice said, "No cracks, Hardin. We mean business. In fourteen minutes, exactly at midnight, go downstairs to the shooting gallery. Go to the right end of the gun counter and look behind the little gate. There'll be a note on the floor. It'll be addressed to you. Don't go one minute early. We're watching and if you do we kill the woman."

Bart said, "What woman?"

"Arlene. Mrs. Maddox Slade. We got her and we mean business. Get that note at midnight." There was a brief pause, then an unpleasant chuckle, and the voice said, "Merry Christmas, Hardin." The phone was dead.

Hardin hung up the receiver. He stood uncertainly. He thought of going downstairs at once and telling Slade. He thought of calling the cops. And in the end he decided to follow the instructions given him by the disguised voice. He had a drink, waited impatiently as the minutes ticked away. He waited for two extra minutes in case his caller's watch was wrong. Then he left his apartment and started down the stairs.

Bromberg, proprietor of the fun arcade, was charging up the stairs and he seemed wildly excited. "Mr. Editor! Mr. Editor!" he screamed at Bart. "Call up your friend, Lieutenant Romano, the homicide man, please! Hurry! A man has just been murdered in my shooting gallery!"

Bart took a firm grip on Bromberg's shoulder, tried to calm him. "Tell me about it," he said. "What man was killed?"

"I do not know," Bromberg cried hysterically. "A customer who was shooting at my sitting ducks. Someone shot him in the back. You could not tell the shot from the exploding rifles, but the man fell down, like he had a heart attack and there was a hole in his back and he is dead. Please call your friend Romano!"

Bart said, "There's no use. If the murder's reported, Homicide at Manhattan West will get it automatically and if Romano is on duty he'll be here. How long ago did it happen?"

"Just now. I called the cops. I flagged a prowl car."

Bart nodded and said, "Let's go downstairs."

Cops were at the doors of the shooting gallery, but there were many doors and Bromberg admitted that any number of people might have left the place before the police arrived. Those who remained were silent and white-faced and had a startled look of shock. Bart noted that Maddox Slade was not among those present.

The body lay on the floor, almost against the gun counter of the shooting gallery. It was at the right of the counter, near the little gate that led to the rear where a bosomy blonde passed out rifles to the customers. Two prowl-car cops Bart knew stood over the body. Bart nodded to them. The body was on its face. There was a hole through the fleece-lined jacket it was wearing. A battered hat was at the side of the body. A target gun hung from the counter by a chain and swung to and fro over the body.

At least, Bart thought, it isn't Maddox Slade.

Bart fished for a cigarette in his pocket, managed to drop the package over the little gate to the rear of the counter. He leaned over the gate to pick up the package, saw the envelope addressed to him lying on the floor. He picked up the cigarette package and the envelope. He slipped the envelope surreptitiously into his pocket.

More police arrived. They were headed by Bart's friend, Lieutenant Romano, and a young detective named Grierson. There were identification men and a harried-looking assistant medical examiner.

Romano was a husky, middle-aged man with a dark Italian face and brooding eyes. He looked sorrowfully at Bart, nodded and said, "Merry Christmas. Even on Christmas it's got to happen. Even on Christmas, people got to go on killing each other."

The medical examiner was bending over the body on

the floor. He handed a wallet up to Romano. Romano sheafed through the wallet.

Bromberg said, "He was shot down just like one of my sitting ducks."

Romano said, "Uh-uh, honey boy. Not a sitting duck. A sitting drake. That's his name according to what's in the wallet. Erik Drake."

three

The medical examiner said, "The bullet went between the second and third ribs, toward the left of the back. We'll probably find it's lodged in the heart. Death, I'd say, was instantaneous, I can make a couple of other guesses. The weapon was a .32 or .38 and it was fired from fifteen or twenty feet, no more."

The tired-looking man rose to his feet, gestured toward one of the several doors to the shooting gallery. It was the door to the hallway that led to the apartments upstairs. "He could have been standing about there. Figure it this way. He had the gun under his coat, concealed by a scarf or handkerchief maybe. He was watching the victim aim the target gun. Just as the victim got ready to pull the trigger, the murderer brought his own gun to bear and shot, too. The sounds would have come right together, and there would have been other guns going off. All the murderer had to do was turn around, go through the door. He was probably down the hall and out in the street before anybody knew what had happened."

The blonde behind the gun counter said, "I remember something now. The little man had been firing at a stationary target, that big sitting duck over on the right. He'd fired three or four times and missed it. Then I saw the duck go down. I was just about to push the lever that sets it up again when I noticed the little man. He was slumping over, like he was sick or something, then he fell down. He kind of slid down the counter."

"So a duck and a drake both got hit," Romano said. He turned to Bromberg. "You notice anybody standing by that door?"

Bromberg said, "I'm pretty sure, Mr. Detective. I think it was there I noticed him. He had a pulled-down hat and a turned-up collar and he looked suspicious."

Bart thought of Maddox Slade.

Romano said, "Can't we have a better description than that?"

Bromberg thought about it. "You couldn't see his face much. A gray hat. A dark coat. A big fellow."

"Young or old?" Hardin asked.

Bromberg shrugged. "I only barely looked at him. It was warm inside and I wondered why he was all bundled up. I wondered why he just stood there instead of playing ski ball or shooting at the ducks. I don't like bums who come inside only to get warm. But he was not a bum. I think I would say he was a young man. That was the impression."

Romano said to Hardin, "Why'd you ask that question, honey boy?"

Bart tried to pass it off. If the man was young, it couldn't have been Maddox Slade. Besides, Slade was a Broadway

38

figure and Bromberg must know him, at least by sight. Bromberg had been on Broadway a long time.

Bart said, "Excuse me. Just trying to be helpful, Lieutenant."

"What were you doing down here?" Romano asked. "You shoot sitting ducks? Or have you got some connection with this business?"

Bart said, "Bromberg called me. He wanted me to phone you, but I told him you'd be here anyway if you were on duty."

Romano nodded, turned to the large young detective whose name was Grierson. He said, "Circulate around among the customers who are left here. You and the other boys ask questions. It never does any good, but it's what the public expects a cop to do. Get addresses, then send 'em home." He looked sadly at Bart. "You know," he said, "I could have taken Christmas off. I got enough years in the department I can make my own schedule for the holidays unless something is breaking. But I wanted to work on account of my health. I got what they call a nervous duodenal and if I'd stayed home I'd have eaten a lot of cookies and candy and turkey stuffing and plum pudding and upset my stomach. I thought things would be quiet on Christmas and I could just rest myself in my little cubbyhole and take bicarb. But murder upsets me even more than turkey stuffing. I should have stayed at home."

Bart said, "You should retire and write your memoirs. That's nice and restful."

"Uh-uh," Romano answered. "Nobody would read 'em.

People expect cops to be brilliant, especially cops on Homicide. But they're not. All they do is plod along and make the gestures they're supposed to make and hope that something breaks."

"I'm no use to you," Bart said. "I got here after it was over. I'm going back upstairs and get some sleep."

He nodded and started toward the door where a murderer had been standing. Romano said, "What's the matter? The gin mills close up early Christmas?"

Bart grinned over his shoulder at Romano and said, "Merry Christmas, Copper."

"Yeah," Romano answered sadly. "Happy New Year, and don't ever join the cops."

As soon as he had bolted the door of his flat, Bart tore open the note that had been tossed on the floor behind the gun counter. It was the same slanted penciling as the note Slade had received by special delivery earlier in the evening. It said:

HARDIN

STAY HOME ON CHRISTMAS TILL YOU RECEIVE A PACKAGE. HAVE SLADE GET 50,000 IN 20s FROM BANK FIRST THING THE 26TH. WE GOT HER AND WE KILL HER IF HE DONT.

Bart sat drumming his fingers on a small telephone table for several moments. Finally he picked up the phone and called Slade's home. Hodgson said Slade had not returned from Midnight Mass. He said that Mrs. Slade was not at home. Yes, Hodgson told Bart, he always waited up

40

for *Mr*. Slade." Apparently he did not wait up for Mrs. Slade. Yes, said Hodgson, he would have Mr. Slade call Mr. Hardin immediately when he came home.

Bart sat for more than an hour in a chair by the window, drinking Irish whiskey and watching the snow fall softly over the glaring desolation of Times Square. Finally the phone rang.

Slade said, breathlessly, "Is she with you, Hardin? Is she all right?"

In as few words as possible, Hardin told Slade of the events of the past few hours.

"You left her alone, Hardin? Why did you do that? Why?" Slade asked accusingly.

Bart was angry, but he realized his anger arose largely from a sense of guilt. His employer had relied upon him to protect a woman who was too intoxicated to protect herself and he had failed. Now his reason for leaving Arlene alone seemed absurd. Good Lord, Bart thought, will I tell the man I was worried about my virtue? He said, rather feebly, "She went sound asleep and I needed cigarettes. While I was out, she must have left."

"Do you think this Erik Drake who was killed is the man who painted the atrocity you saw here?" Slade asked.

Hardin said, "I wouldn't know. It's a fairly unusual name, but it could be a coincidence, I suppose. Didn't you recognize him? You must have seen him."

There was silence on the line, then Slade said, "What on earth are you implying, Hardin? I've never met this artist or any of Arlene's bohemian friends. And what do you mean by saying I must have seen him?"

Hardin said, "You were in the shooting gallery just a few minutes before it happened."

Hardin could hear Slade's breath exhale in a long sigh. Finally he said, "I was seen there, then?"

"I passed the door and saw you when I glanced in," Bart answered. "Bromberg has sharp eyes and he must know you by sight, but he didn't mention seeing you."

Slade said, "I found a notation on the floor in Arlene's handwriting. It must have fallen from her purse. It indicated she had a rendezvous at this fun arcade at midnight. She's been acting very strangely recently. I went there before midnight, looked around, waited awhile. Then there was some excitement up by the shooting gallery. I thought a man had fainted. I didn't want to be noticed. I slipped out the street door on Forty-second Street and walked to the Church of the Theatre and attended Midnight Mass as I always do on Christmas Eve."

Bart asked, "Was it the door to the street or the door to the hallway you left by?"

"The big door that opens directly on the street," said Slade. "Why do you ask?"

"Because the police may be asking if they find you were there and that there's even a vague connection between you and Drake. Did anyone see you at Mass?"

"I had to stand up in back because I arrived late, but I nodded to a few acquaintances. They may remember."

Bart said, "It may still be a bluff or some elaborate practical joke. But murder's not humorous. It seems the only way that I can serve is sit and wait. I'll sit and wait, all over Christmas, if I have to. The *Broadway Times* comes out on Christmas like any other day but I can have old Pops Taylor cover me if the package hasn't arrived by noon when it's time to go to work. I'll call you if there's a break. Maybe you'd better stay home, too, just in case they decide to call you or send you another Christmas card. Of course, we *could* go to the cops. That might even be the best way."

"No!" Slade cried hysterically. "No, Hardin, don't dare do that. You haven't any right. It's my wife's life that's at stake. I'll get them the money. I'll pay them anything, anything."

"In that case," Bart said, "I'll sit and wait for orders or whatever Christmas gift is in the package."

He hung up. He didn't feel like getting drunk alone and there was nothing else to do, so he went to bed. His sleep was troubled. Twice Slade called to say that Arlene had not returned and to ask Bart if he had heard anything from the kidnappers. Slade's second call came at five in the morning. Bart's eyes were gummed with sleep as he answered the phone, but he noted that snow was still falling outside the smeared windowpanes.

It was nine-thirty before he was awakened again. This time it was not the phone. It was a clamorous knocking on the heavy door of his apartment. There was no doorbell. The street door for the upper quarters of the fun arcade and the flats above was never locked, since Bromberg's tenants were unconventional people who kept unconventional hours and frequently lost their keys. Bart went to the door of the apartment and opened it.

Santa Claus said, "Merry Christmas, sir."

Santa Claus was conventionally fat and his nose was small and red but his eyes did not twinkle in the way that Clement Moore had described them. The eyes were bloodshot and bleary with an alcoholic hangover. There was a gray stubble of beard on Santa Claus's weatherbeaten face, but the long white whiskers protruded from a large patch pocket of his bright red suit. The snout of a bottle was sticking out of the same pocket.

Bart said, "Merry Christmas. How'd you miss the chimney?"

Santa Claus was carrying a gift-wrapped package tied with bright gold ribbon. The paper was unusual. It was silver with an abstract pattern that vaguely resembled green fir trees.

Santa Claus chuckled. He said, "The shape I'm in, boss, I could hardly make the door. Please, mister, what's your name?"

Bart said, "Hardin, Bart Hardin. Why?"

"Because I've got a great big package here for a good little boy named Bart Hardin," Santa Claus answered. "A package to be delivered in person by old Santy himself." He extended the large, gift-wrapped box to Hardin.

Hardin took the package and said, "Thank you. But there doesn't seem to be a card. Who sent it?"

"Maybe there's a card inside," Santa Claus answered. "I don't know the little lady's name. All I know is she asked me to deliver the package to somebody named Bart Hardin at this address."

Bart said, "You look as if you could use a shot. Why

don't you come inside and sit down a minute. You can tell me all about it while you're having a drink."

Santa said, "Mister, them's the nicest words that anybody's said to me this Christmas." He entered the apartment and took a chair. Bart poured a stiff drink of Irish into a tumbler, handed it to Santa Claus. "What's your name?" he asked.

Santa Claus said, "You mean my *square* name, mister? Nobody remembers that any more. Where I hang out nobody's got a square name. It's Melvin Holtzheimer, in case you really want to know. But if you ever want to get in touch with me, you ask around for Old Fats at the Palace gin mill or the Castle Rooms on the Bowery. Old Fats, that's what they call me. If you don't find me at either of them places, likely they'll know about me at the Mission. I ain't a Mission stiff but I go there sometime when things are tough. I ain't a bum. I'm a 'bo. There's a difference. A bum won't never work. A 'bo will —sometimes, anyway. I been a gandy dancer and a dishwasher and I get this Santa Claus job with the Volunteers of America every Christmas. They like me because I'm fat and it ain't necessary to use no stuffing in the red suit."

Bart said, "I thought all Santa Clauses went off duty Christmas Eve."

Old Fats nodded gravely, smacked his lips over the whiskey. "Man, this beats canned heat and Sneaky Pete a mile," he said. "Last night around nine o'clock the lieutenant from the Volunteers come around with the little truck and picked up the chimney box that people

45

drop their money in and he took the dinner bell I ring and give me a slip of paper and told me to go down to East Houston and pick up the pay was coming to me and turn in my uniform. But I made a big mistake. I stopped off for a couple of beers at a joint on Eighth Avenue and there was some sports in there thought it was funny having Santa Claus in a gin mill and they started buying me drinks till they was piled up in front of me on the bar. Then they took me around with them to see some friends of theirs in hotel rooms and apartments and we had a drink everywhere we went and finally I wind up in a flophouse on Ninth Avenue not even knowing how I got there, still dressed up like Santy. I didn't even have a subway token when I woke up so I started walking and when I got to Forty-second and Eighth, about, I meet this nice little old lady."

Bart poured another drink for Santa Claus, laid a five-dollar bill beside it and said, "Here's a little something for your trouble. Tell me all about this lady."

Santa said, "You're a real sport, mister. This is the luckiest Christmas Old Fats ever had. She was a widow lady, I guess, and she was crippled a little bit. Anyway, she walked with a limp. She was dressed all in black with one of them widow veils over her face, so I couldn't see what she looked like much, except she was small. She had this package and she stopped me. She said she was going to deliver this Christmas present to a friend of hers but she thought it would be a fine idea to have Santa Claus deliver it instead—and she slipped me five bucks and give me your name and told me to bring the package.

She waited till she saw me come in the building, and I guess that's all there is to it."

"Can't you tell me more about her? Describe her better?"

Old Fats said, "I'm sorry, mister. I didn't hang around. I was afraid she might change her mind and a fin's a lot of cabbage to an old 'bo like me." His brow wrinkled. Obviously he wanted to earn Bart's five, too. He said, "She was kind of short, something around five-three, about. But she wasn't skinny. I couldn't hardly see her face behind this veil, except it was pale and old-looking."

"You think you could identify her if you saw her again?"

Suspicion had come into Santa Claus's bleary eyes. "There ain't nothing wrong, is there, mister?" he asked. "There ain't no law in this, is there? I don't want no law. All it was, a lady asked me to do an errand and she paid me and I did it."

Bart said, "There's nothing to worry about. It's just a joke. But there could be some more dough in it for you if you could identify her, maybe."

Melvin Holtzheimer was obviously wrestling with his conscience. He said, "I—I could try. If she was dressed just the same, maybe I could. But if you want the plain truth, I didn't get too good a look at her, not in all them widow weeds and veils and things. She was kind of— shapeless—and she talked in a cracked kind of way like she had a bad cold or was kind of whispering."

Bart said, "Well, thanks for the present. The five's yours. If you remember anything else, call this number."

He jotted down his phone number on a piece of paper, handed it to the old man.

Old Fats nodded. "I will, mister. You're a real sport. Maybe you could let me have just one more touch of the old sauce before I go out into the cold."

Bart grinned, poured Santa Claus one for the road. Old Fats swallowed it at a gulp, coughed and mumbled fervent thanks as he left the flat.

Hardin made sure the door was locked after his boozy Father Christmas left. Then he opened the package. Beneath the silver paper with the abstract fir trees was a large, plain cardboard box. Inside that was a brief case, a theatre ticket and an envelope. The brief case was capacious and cheap. It was made of plastic which was crinkled to simulate alligator hide. The theatre ticket and the letter were inside the brief case. The ticket was for seat 102, Row L, of the December 26 performance of Tennessee Williams' *Camino Réal* at the Opportunity, Incorporated Theatre on Bleecker Street. The envelope was addressed "Bart Hardin" in the slanted penciled capitals that had become so familiar to Bart within the past few hours. Several ruled tablet sheets were inside and the message on them was written in the same penciled printing.

HARDIN

WOMAN SAFE. SHE STAYS SAFE IF YOU AND SLADE FOLLOW INSTRUCTIONS.

1. SLADE GETS $50,000 IN 20s OUT OF BANK. PUT MONEY IN BRIEF CASE.

2. HARDIN TAKES BRIEF CASE TO THEATRE AND
USES ENCLOSED TICKET. PUT BRIEF CASE WITH
MONEY UNDER SEAT.

3. HARDIN GETS TO THEATRE 8:40 EXACTLY. GET
READY TO LEAVE NEAR END OF SCENE 2, ACT 1,
WHEN KILROY ENTERS AND LIGHTS DIM. SHOULD BE
LEAVING THEATRE WHEN GUTMAN SAYS, "BLOCK
THREE ON THE CAMINO RÉAL." DON'T LOOK BACK
DON'T RETURN TO THEATRE. LEAVE BRIEF CASE
UNDER SEAT.

4. DON'T NOTIFY POLICE OR ANYBODY AND DON'T
MARK MONEY.

5. DON'T TRY TO SET TRAP.

6. WOMAN FREE IN ONE HOUR IF INSTRUCTIONS
FOLLOWED.

There was nothing inscrutable about the message to
Bart. He had seen *Camino Réal* several times during its
brief run on Broadway and had considered the symbolic,
offbeat fantasy one of the greatest theatrical experiences
of his time. He had lost all respect for the drama critics,
including the drama critic of the *Broadway Times,* who
had called it "obscure" and frightened playgoers away
from it. The play, he knew, dealt with a mythical town
in a wasteland inhabited by such frustrated romantics
as Jacques Casanova, Marguerite Gautier, Baron de
Charlus, Lord Byron and Don Quixote. Toward the end
of Scene 2, Bart recalled, there bursts into this unlikely
company the star of the play, a muscular young American
prizefighter by the name of Kilroy. Gutman, the other

49

character mentioned in the note, is a cynical innkeeper who comments caustically on the behavior of his guests and who ends each scene with the announcement that another block of the road called the *Camino Réal,* which is symbolic of the time-stream, has been traversed. Immediately after such announcements the lights are lowered and the theatre is in temporary darkness. That fact would enable Bart to leave unnoticed and would enable the kidnapper to pick up the brief case containing fifty thousand dollars.

Hardin read the note over several times. Then he examined the theatre ticket. "Complimentary" was stamped across the front. If the theatre was as small as other off-Broadway houses, his row would be the twelfth, probably the last row. And if seats were numbered as they were in some Broadway houses, his reservation was on the aisle. It was a convenient arrangement.

Hardin picked up the phone and called Slade. He said, "I don't think I'd better tell you too much over the phone. I received the Christmas package. The lady is safe, I understand. I have certain instructions. I'll tell you all about it as soon as I can dress and eat some breakfast and get up there."

Slade protested. His usually unctuous voice was sharp and frantic. He was full of questions, but Bart cut him short.

"I'll skip breakfast," he said. "Maybe Hodgson can get me something to eat. I'll be there in forty-five minutes or less."

But he was later than that in arriving.

As he was leaving the apartment there was another knock on the door. Bart's second guest was also bleary-eyed, but he wasn't dressed as Santa Claus.

When Bart opened the door he faced Lieutenant Romano. The swarthy detective seemed dead-tired. His heavy shoulders were stooped, his collar was crumpled, his eyes were bloodshot and his battered felt was on the back of his head as usual.

Romano said, "Hello, honey boy. You leaving this early? I didn't think you went to work till noon. I've got things to ask about."

Romano walked past Bart, dropped wearily into a chair. Bart said, "You look beat. You want a drink for breakfast? I don't have any Wheaties."

Romano shook his head. "It's too early. Besides, I don't like the sharp edge of that Irish you drink. It burns my stomach. I might be tempted if you drank the same booze your daddy used to keep around when he was alive. That bourbon he had was old enough to vote."

Romano put his hand to his mouth to stifle a burp and said, "Excuse me. I don't sleep or eat right when a murder's breaking and my duodenal gets more nervous. This guy who got shot was a kind of artist. He lived in Greenwich Village and he painted funny-looking pictures. He also was a set designer for one of those little theatres called Opportunity, Incorporated. You know anybody lives in Gracie Square?"

The sudden question startled Bart, but he tried not to

let surprise show on his face. He said, "I don't number the big rich among my more intimate friends, but the boss lives up there. Slade. I've been to his apartment."

"Yeah, that's right," Romano said, conversationally. He took a little tin box from his pocket, flipped an antacid tablet into his mouth, let it dissolve on his tongue as he continued to speak. "Number 22. We found a little slip of paper in the pocket of the guy who got shot. It said '22 Gracie Square.' "

Bart said, "It's a big apartment house. The one on the river. A lot of people live in it."

"Yeah," Romano said. "Only most of them weren't in Bromberg's shooting gallery last night. Slade was."

"What makes you think that?"

"Bromberg. The little man with the spit curl. Slade's a big wheel on Broadway. He gets his pictures in the paper. Bromberg saw him in the shooting gallery just before the murder. You got any idea why Mr. Slade should go to a shooting gallery on Christmas Eve?"

Bart said, "I wouldn't know. He's quite a sportsman. Maybe he was practicing up for the grouse season."

"Could be, I guess," Romano answered. "Or maybe he was shooting ducks and Drakes."

four

"I remember Bromberg mentioned a man with a turned-up collar and turned-down hat," Bart said. "He thought he was suspicious. But he also said the man was young. Nobody could call Slade young."

"That was another man," Romano answered. "We got all kinds of mysterious people all over the place, the way it happens in the books. He says this Slade had his hat turned down and his coat turned up, too. But he wasn't standing by the door to the hallway. He was over by the street door. And Bromberg didn't notice him right at the time of the murder. He noticed him a few minutes before, he thinks."

Bart said, "That should let Slade out so far as shooting Drake is concerned. The Medical Examiner guessed the shot was fired from no more than twenty feet. It's fifty or sixty feet at least from the shooting gallery to the street door."

"He could have moved," Romano answered.

"But why on earth should you think a man like Slade would shoot somebody like this Drake?"

"I didn't say I thought he did. I only said there's a connection. Item one, this Drake had the address of Slade's house inside his pocket when he got bumped. Item two, I been making a nuisance of myself and asking questions. It's a habit I've got that makes some people mad. I asked questions of a funny little guy with a bald head and a Vandyke beard down in the Village. He runs the Opportunity, Incorporated Theatre. His name is Carberry Payne. This Payne tells me he's got an actor named Howard Barnaby and that Mrs. Slade used to be friendly with Barnaby. He tells me that Barnaby and Drake used to live together. He tells me that Drake did the sets for the show he's putting on. He also tells me that Mrs. Slade paid this Drake a whopping big amount of dough for a picture he painted just recently. It don't add up to much, but it must add up to something."

"You think Slade would kill a man because his wife bought a picture that he painted?" Bart asked.

Romano said, "Maybe he's an art critic. Maybe it was a lousy picture. And I quit thinking a long time ago. Cops who think wind up in the psycho ward. I just keep digging and sometimes something pops."

Hardin was silent for a moment, his pale eyes searching the lieutenant's sleepy face. Finally he said, "Look, Copper. I like you. I like you because you're one of the few completely honest men I ever met on Broadway. Don't lead with your chin. Slade's a powerful man in this town. There's some easy explanation of all this. There's got to be. If you annoy Slade uselessly he can put the needle in places where it'll hurt. He knows the commissioner personally, for one thing."

54

"Yeah," Romano answered. "I've annoyed a lot of powerful people, although I don't enjoy it much. It's just my job. Sometimes I've annoyed them so much they've landed in the electric chair."

Hardin said, "Slade won't take it sitting down. Not in any kind of chair."

Romano sighed and stifled another burp behind his fine Italian hand. "Don't scare me, honey boy," he said. "It makes my stomach nervous and I got enough grief already."

"Have you questioned Slade?"

"Uh-uh. But I've got to. I've got the rank, so that means I'm the one who has to lead with his chin, like you say, and annoy the ones who can make trouble. I can leave the other ones to Grierson, because he's just a first-grade detective and I'm a lieutenant. He's already seen this Barnaby. Made him mad as hell by getting him out of bed before seven o'clock this morning. He claimed that was the first he'd heard of the murder. He says he and this Drake broke up housekeeping a few weeks ago. Says Drake objected to him because he messed up the apartment, throwing his clothes around and burning the furniture with cigarettes. He thinks the little guy was an old-maid type. He admitted he'd known Mrs. Slade before her marriage, but claims it was what they call platonic. Said she was interested in young actors and tried to help him was all. Barnaby's got an alibi. Claims he went right from the theatre to his girl friend's apartment. Grierson also got the girl friend out of bed. Her name's Brent, Violet Brent. She's young and she does some acting around this Opportunity, Incorporated place. Claims Barnaby took her home right after the show last night and stayed in her apartment till three o'clock. Says they made fudge and decorated a little Christmas tree. Grierson says she's real young and sweet and it's hard not to believe her. Says she didn't even bawl him out for getting her out of bed around seven-thirty."

"When are you interviewing Slade?" Bart asked.

"I'm on my way there now. I thought maybe you'd like to go along, since he's your boss."

Bart said, "No. I've got to get dressed, eat some breakfast and go to work. Newspapermen are like cops. They work on Christmas."

Romano nodded. "Yeah," he said. "I figured you would want to call and warn him that I'm coming. After all, he's your boss. But I came here anyway because I thought there might be some easy explanation of this thing and you might know it, since you work for Slade. I don't like leading with my chin unless it's necessary. I may be a chump, but I'm not that honest." He rose, sighed, struggled into his coat. "Okay, Editor. You can reach for the phone now. I'm leaving to see a millionaire."

At the door, Romano turned, grinned at Bart. "How do you get to be a millionaire?" he asked. He thought about it and said, "I guess it's easy, really. All you do is make a million bucks."

The lieutenant opened the heavy door, closed it carefully behind him. Bart picked up the phone immediately.

Slade's voice was angry. He said, "Hardin? I don't like

this. I don't like your attitude. You're taking this thing almost casually. You should have been here by now, before this. Don't you realize what I'm going through?"

Bart said curtly, "Never mind that now. You're in trouble. A homicide man is on his way to see you, and don't be fooled by his sleepy look. You know him. It's Romano, and he's one of the smartest cops in town."

Bart told his employer what Romano knew. He did not mention Howard Barnaby, however. There was no use in bringing that up in case Slade did not know of Arlene's affair with the young man.

Slade said, his voice pathetically pleading now, "What will I do, Hardin? What on earth will I tell this man?"

"I'll give you advice," Hardin answered. "But I doubt you'll take it. Tell the truth. Tell him about the kidnapping. The kidnapping is almost certainly tied up with Drake's murder."

"Hardin!" Slade exclaimed. "You're asking me to sign Arlene's death warrant! How can you even suggest such a thing?"

"I don't think there's any real risk," Bart said. "There's one thing I'm sure of. These people aren't professionals. They're clever but they're rank amateurs. The cops and the F.B.I. could catch them in a few hours if we give them the facts and hold nothing back."

"No!" Slade exclaimed. "I'll never forgive you if you talk, Hardin. My wife's life is at stake and these 'people' you mention may have committed a murder already. They won't hesitate to commit another one. I'm going to run, Hardin. I'm going to tell Hodgson to inform this detective that Arlene and I are out of town for Christmas and won't return until tomorrow night. They don't have enough on me to get a warrant out. They'll wait that long. And by tomorrow night the ransom will be paid and Arlene will be safe and we can tell them everything. I'm going to a little family hotel I know up by Columbia University. I stayed there once before when there was a business reason for making myself unavailable. They know me under the name of Carter. I'm leaving now, Hardin, before this detective gets here. Hodgson can bring my bag later. You stay by your phone until I call. I want to see you. Remember the name I'll use. Carter."

Bart said, "It's your . . ."

He choked off the sentence. He had almost said "Funeral." It was hardly a discreet word to use under the present circumstances.

"It's your affair," he wound up lamely.

Slade said, "Wait, Hardin. Wait there by the phone. You should hear from me inside an hour." He rang off.

Well, Hardin thought, that's one way to meet a crisis. You just run from it. Maybe that's what's the matter with the world. We've been running too fast too long and getting nowhere. Then he smiled bitterly. If he hadn't run away himself the night before, Arlene wouldn't have been kidnapped. Hardin didn't like himself at all as he showered and shaved and finally donned his clothes. Maybe I'm not in my right mind, any more than Slade is, he thought as he buttoned up his shirt. But at least I'll be fully clothed.

Before the hour was up Slade called. His voice was

hushed almost to a whisper as Bart answered the phone. "Hardin, this is Carter. Are you alone?"

Bart said, "I'm alone, Mr. Carter."

"I have to see you right away. I'm in the Thackeray Hotel on One Hundred and Fourteenth Street, just west of Broadway. Suite 483. Can you come right up?"

Bart said, "I'm on my way."

Hardin flagged a cab on Forty-second Street. The snow had turned to a slow, insistent rain and Broadway was ankle-deep in muddy slush. There was little traffic but the heap jockey drove slowly over the slippery streets. The hotel was a brick building, small, sedate and old-fashioned. Bart imagined its tenants were drawn mostly from the students and faculty members of the neighboring university. It was hardly the place that a pretentious man like Slade would choose even for a brief residence. Bart doubted Slade had used the hideaway before because of any business emergencies that demanded his temporary disappearance. Slade had rather prided himself on his reputation as a gay blade in his bachelor days and this place could have served as a convenient retreat for him and any of his numerous "protégées."

There was a prissy-looking little clerk behind the desk in the tiny lobby. He was occupied in tying a red ribbon around a tissue-wrapped package and he did not challenge Bart. Hardin waited for nearly five minutes and pushed the bell several times before an ancient elevator in an open-work cage descended from the upper reaches. A sad-looking Negro in a lumberjack shirt finally piloted him to the fourth floor.

Slade opened the door a crack and peered out cautiously when Hardin rapped on the panel of 483. It was ludicrous and at the same time it was pitiful to see this usually self-assured, money-powerful man in a state that bordered upon abject fear. Bart wondered if something more than Arlene's disappearance could account for the state of Slade's nerves. His face was no longer ruddy. It was the dirty gray of the slush on Broadway. His lips trembled slightly when he spoke and his voice was not the hearty, overbearing voice of Maddox Slade. It was pleading, almost whining.

Slade said, "Tell me, Hardin. Tell me everything about Arlene. Then we can discuss this other matter."

Hardin told his employer of the visit he had received from Santa Claus. He had brought the brief case along. He showed that and the ransom note and the theatre ticket to Slade. He said, "I still say we should go to the police."

"How can you possibly say that?" Slade demanded, anger in his face now, his voice almost shrill. "I repeat, Hardin, I don't like your attitude. I haven't liked it from the first. You seem to have no concern at all for Arlene's safety, which is the only thing that really matters. You left her alone there in your apartment last night after I had asked you to watch out for her. And now you suggest I do the one thing the kidnappers warn us not to do—go to the police. This is fantastic. Don't you realize this is a desperate situation? Have you no sympathy at all for me and what I'm going through?"

Maybe it's a good thing he's angry, Hardin thought.

At least some color is coming back into his face. He said, "I'm sorry. I made a mistake when I left your wife alone last night, but I had no way of knowing then that she was in danger. You didn't take the first kidnap note seriously. Neither did I. I'm thinking of her safety when I say we should call the cops. These people are **amateurs**. You and I can't deal with them. But professionals—the police, the F.B.I.—can deal with them, and beat them."

"Why on earth do you insist they're amateurs?" Slade asked. "This is a devilishly clever plan. It's well worked out to the last detail. There's a clever, brutal mind behind this, Hardin."

"It's clever on the surface," Hardin admitted. "But they've made mistakes experienced criminals would never make. They bungled the timing of the first kidnap note and almost ruined the thing before it even started. They've given us all the time in the world to make plans to catch them. Almost two full days. Professionals would never have done that. They took a big chance in delivering the brief case the way they did. One of their people had to come almost to my door and she had to risk approaching a stranger who might be able to identify her later. Professionals would never have risked such a close personal contact as that. And they had to depend on a stranger, a Bowery bum, to deliver the case and the note and the ticket to me. The woman watched him go into the house but she would hardly have dared to wait around until he came out again. He was a bum. He already had her five bucks. He might have thought the package was worth something and just waited in the hallway until she left and kept it himself. They've left too much to chance. And the biggest mistake of all is giving us the time to list the serial numbers of the ransom bills. That's the way dozens of kidnappers, including Hauptmann, have been caught. There's no doubt in my mind that they're amateurs. Incompetent amateurs at that."

The color was fading from Slade's face again. "Theories are fine," he said at length. "You may even be right. But I can't possibly take a chance. It would be like murdering my own wife to go to the police. I won't do it, Hardin. You're a stubborn man, I know that. But for God's sake, promise me that you won't mention this to the police, to anybody, that you'll follow their instructions to the letter."

Hardin said, "If that's the way you want it, that's the way I'll play it. But this murder is a complication. Romano knows you were in the shooting gallery. He knows Arlene bought that picture of the ducks. He wants to talk to both of you. He's a digger. He won't stop digging until he finds you."

"He won't find me," Slade declared, some of his old assurance returning to him. "Not before tomorrow night, anyway. And by then this nightmare will be ended."

"You can't just stay here locked up in this room," Bart told him. "You have to go to the bank tomorrow and draw the ransom money."

Slade was regaining his composure rapidly, Bart thought. The look of indulgent contempt for lesser men, an expression familiar to Hardin, had come into his face. "I have thought of that, of course," Slade said. "It can be arranged, with a little help from you. The president of my bank, the Brokers Trust, is an old and intimate friend. There is a pay phone in the lobby of this hotel. I am going down there and call him at his home in Long Island. He will make the necessary arrangements and will ask no questions. He will think it is a business emergency. He may think it odd that I want the money in bills of such denominations, but he is a discreet man and he can be trusted. I will describe you and tell him you will pick the money up for me. I have already made out the draft." He handed a sealed envelope to Hardin. "The draft is drawn and signed," he said. "You will find it inside the envelope when you need it." He looked at Hardin appraisingly. "You see," he said, "I am trusting you with fifty thousand dollars. I hope I am not putting temptation in your path."

Hardin pocketed the envelope without looking inside.

There was a gentle, barely audible knocking on the door.

Slade jerked nervously from his chair and his face went pale. Hardin went to the door, opened it a crack, feeling rather foolish. Hodgson, Slade's man, was outside the door, dressed in the correct garb of a gentleman's gentleman, even to bowler hat and umbrella. He was carrying a large package in Christmas wrapping.

Slade said, "Are you sure you weren't followed?"

"Certainly, sir," Hodgson answered, placing the package on a table and removing his bowler. "I took great precautions. I felt it possible they might watch the house and be suspicious if I left with a suitcase. So I packed your fresh linen and necessities in this box and wrapped it as a Christmas present. I came here by a most circuitous route. The journey has taken me well over an hour. I can swear that no one followed me."

Slade said, "Thank you, Hodgson. That was clever of you."

"I'm afraid that I'm not clever, sir," Hodgson answered modestly. "Merely cautious."

"You saw this detective?" Slade asked.

"Yes, sir. He was most persistent and most suspicious."

"What did you tell him?"

"Just what you said, sir. That you and Mrs. Slade had left late last night and were motoring to a retreat in the country for Christmas. I told him that since you did not wish to be disturbed you had left no address or phone number and that I did not know your destination."

"You say he was suspicious?"

"I'm afraid so, sir. He forced his way into the apartment, although I must say he did so most politely. He examined the cigar you had been smoking. It was in an ash tray in the living room. He seemed to find that it was warm. He asked me if I was in the habit of sitting in the living room and smoking my employer's cigars when he was not home. I told him I was sometimes guilty of doing so."

"What did he say to that?"

"He—he said, sir, that I should not smoke cigars. He said they caused a nervous condition of the stomach."

Slade said, "You acted properly, Hodgson. As usual. Thank you."

"Not at all, sir," Hodgson replied. "And begging your pardon, I have taken the liberty of closing the house until your return. You may remember you gave me the afternoon and evening off to visit my niece on Staten Island, since you and Mrs. Slade had planned to have Christmas goose at Luchow's Restaurant. I thought my absence might avoid any further inquiries."

Slade nodded. "Yes. That's the best way all around. Leave me your niece's phone number. I'll call you when you're needed."

"I have already taken the liberty of writing it down, sir," said the efficient Hodgson, producing a neatly lettered card from the pocket of his vest and laying it on the table beside the box of clothes.

"You may go now, Hodgson," Slade said. "I can't explain this temporary difficulty to you right now, but it's nothing serious and I trust you will use your usual discretion and not discuss it. And I hope all this has not marred your Christmas."

Hodgson tucked the umbrella under his arm and raised the bowler toward his head. "It is not my place to ask questions or to discuss your affairs, sir," he said. "And Christmas is just another day."

He left, closing the door silently behind him.

Hardin said, "It's afternoon and I've got a paper to put out. Also, I haven't even eaten breakfast yet. If you've got more instructions, you'd better give them to me now, so I can get to work."

Slade regarded Hardin for a long time without speaking, his eyes narrowed and contemplative. At length he said, "You're not being entirely honest with me. You know more about this than you've told me, I'm sure of that."

Hardin made no answer. What does he want me to tell him? he asked himself. That I left his wife alone because I thought she might make a pass at me while she was blotto? That his wife was being blackmailed because she played around with a twenty-three-year-old kid?

Hardin met Slade's suspicious eyes. He said, "Let's understand each other. I don't like this, but I'll go through with it. I think it's the wrong way, but I'll take your orders. You blame me for this, I know, because I left your wife alone in my apartment. It was a big mistake, as things turned out, I admit that. You think I was callous because I went out to get a pack of cigarettes and left her there asleep. You know I didn't leave for cigarettes. You know why I left. You know I didn't want to be alone with her in my apartment when she was in that condition and you know the reason why."

Slade took it with no show of emotion. He said, "All this is beside the point now. I have to trust you. I trusted your father for many, many years and he was always worthy of my trust. I held his job open for you when he died while you were fighting in Korea. I've never had reason to regret it—up to now. We've had our little disagreements. You have your faults. You're too hard and cynical in some ways and you're too soft in others. You have too little respect for the really big people of Broadway, the ones who run the show. You have too much tol-

66

erance and pity for the failures, the bums, the alcoholics, the weaklings. But all that's beside the question now, too. I have to trust you, that's the fact. I'm trusting you with my wife's life." There was a new note in Slade's voice now, hard, almost menacing. "Bring her back to me, Hardin. Do anything you have to do, but bring her back. Don't fail. I'm an even-tempered man, but I can be ruthless with men who fail me."

Hardin tried to keep the astonishment he felt from showing on his face. My God, he thought, this man actually thinks I'm implicated in the kidnapping of his wife. He's willing to pay me fifty thousand dollars to get her back, but he's convinced that I'm a kidnapper. It shows all over him.

Hardin rose abruptly, donned his trench coat and said, "Who is it I see tomorrow to get this money?"

"Mr. Gerald Swayne," Slade answered. "Go to the Brokers Trust on Fifth Avenue and Forty-fifth between nine and ten. He'll have the money for you in his office. Send in your name."

' I'll bring the money here and you and I will list the serial numbers, even if it takes all day," Bart said.

He picked up the brief case and walked to the door.

"Don't you think all that's superflous?" Slade asked.

"I think it's absolutely necessary," Hardin answered curtiy. He left without a good-bye and slammed the door behind him.

He was walking toward the elevator when Slade opened the door and beckoned him back.

"If you have to call me here, use a pay booth," Slade said. "The police may tap your phone."

"They won't tap it," Hardin said. "Romano doesn't have to trust me, but ironically enough, he does."

five

Hardin stopped his cab at the Copper Skillet Restaurant. Inside, he entered a phone booth and called Pops Taylor, the turf editor of the *Broadway Times,* who was second in command in the city room. He said, "I don't have to tell you I'll be late because I already am. I'm taking on some fodder and I'll be there as soon as I've finished."

The old man answered, "Take your time. Only you got a guest. Romano, the demon sleuth. He's been sitting in your office quite a while."

"Don't tell him I called," Bart said. "Just let him sit. Cops need excuses to rest their feet."

He ate a Christmas brunch of ham and eggs with three cups of black coffee, overtipped the waitress because she was a frustrated, stage-struck girl who'd never got the break she'd waited for ten years. He walked out into the steady rain and frothy muck of Broadway's Christmas. He walked up Jacobs Beach, turned right on Eighth Avenue at Madison Square Garden. At Fifty-first was the old brick building that housed the *Broadway Times,* an abandoned firehouse that bore the legend "Erected 1882."

Bart found Pops Taylor sitting in his creaky swivel chair in the slot of the horseshoe copy desk that circled around the brass pole, a relic of the building's former tenants.

"Anything breaking?" Bart asked.

The old man scratched his pink, bald scalp with a copy pencil and peered at Bart over his half-moon glasses. "Nothing but the toys the kiddies got for Christmas," he answered. "Your guest was sound asleep the last time I looked in."

"He needs rest," Bart said. "Cops lead a rugged life. You got a hot horse for me to lose my cabbage on?"

"Not today," Pop answered. "I never give out tips on Christmas. But every hunch player on the street will blow his dough on that Santy's Panties in the Christmas Handicap at Florida. Wish I could book the bum. He couldn't get nine furlongs with a jet rocket up his tail."

Bart crossed the cavernous city room to the beaver-boarded cubbyhole he called an office. Romano was sitting at Bart's desk. His eyes were shut and he was breathing through his mouth. His shoes were on the floor beside him and his stockinged feet were propped up on a ledge of the battered roll-top desk.

Bart said, "Merry Christmas, Copper."

Romano opened his heavy-lidded eyes and said, "Merry Christmas, Editor. You got a right comfortable chair. I caught myself a nap."

As Bart was hanging up his coat and hat, Romano put his shoes on, groaning slightly. He rose and sat down again in a straight chair beside the desk. "You're real late to work," he said. "And you were in a bang-up rush to get here when I left you early this morning."

Bart said, "I was delayed."

"You get in touch with Slade all right?" the lieutenant asked innocently.

Bart sat in the swivel chair Romano had just vacated.

"I understand Slade's out of town," Bart replied.

"Words," said Romano. "Words are the damnedest things. You can say them and they sound all right and they don't mean anything at all. You take those words you just said, for instance. They're not a lie and they're not necessarily the truth, either. Now, I could ask you a lot of questions and keep on narrowing it down and pretty soon I'd have you where the words you said would have to be the truth or would have to be a lie. It's a kind of game, but I don't enjoy playing it too much. I don't enjoy making a man lie when he's decided he won't talk. It doesn't do any good, when you come right down to it."

"You're using a lot of words yourself and they don't mean much," Bart said. "You think Slade's in town?"

"I *understand* he's out of town," Romano answered. "At least that little man of his named Hodgson says so. I think the little man is telling me a big, fat lie, though."

"Are you sure?" Bart asked.

"I'm too damned old to be sure about anything any more," Romano answered. "Thursday nights around eleven, that's the worst time. That's when they usually electrocute 'em up at Sing Sing. When one of my boys is up there and it gets to be around ten-thirty I start asking myself, 'Are you sure?' and the more I think about it, the less sure I get, although I've been sure as hell right up to then. By eleven o'clock my nervous stomach is doing flip-flops."

Bart picked up a sheaf of race-horse past-performance proofs the galley boy had tossed on his desk and began to scan them without really seeing them.

Romano said, "You've clammed up. There were a lot of things I intended to ask you, but there's no use wasting my breath, I guess. Come right down to it, breath's about the most important thing there is. You don't have it, you don't live very long. I'll tell you something I'm pretty sure about right now, though. I'm pretty sure you're sore about something. You're all burned up inside. You weren't that way this morning, so it must be something that happened just a little while ago. If you wanted to tell me about it, I'd be glad to listen. You might not believe it, but cops help people sometimes. Even dumb cops like me."

Bart said, "Thanks. I'm not sore at anybody. It's Christmas."

"You've clammed up," Romano said, rising. "I never was much good at opening clams." He took his rumpled blue overcoat from the clothes tree, tucked it carelessly under his arm.

He stood for a moment looking down at Hardin. "I'd like to leave a message with you," he said. "A message for this Slade, just in case you should run into him. Tell him he's too smart a man to act this way. I don't really think he killed that little guy, but I want to talk to him.

If he was cheating on his wife in a shooting gallery or something, I'll keep it quiet. But it would be right nice of him to call me up."

"If I see him, I'll tell him that," Bart promised.

Romano started for the door, his overcoat trailing on the floor behind him. "I waited here about two hours for you," he said. "I didn't get much information, but I had a real nice nap."

Hardin tried to put drunken women, suspicious husbands, abstract artists, muscular young actors, blackmailers, kidnappers and Santa Clauses with alcoholic breaths out of his mind. He had work to do. For more than an hour he concerned himself with reading copy, writing heads and padding out items for the Big Street gossip column that appeared on page one of the paper. Copy boys threw sheets of grayish paper with double-spaced typing on his desk. Ink-grimed galley boys tossed him proofs still wet from the roller. The composing-room skipper called to complain that the drama critic's column was late as usual and old Pops Taylor ambled in with the news that the Daily Double in Florida had paid more than a thousand dollars. It was Christmas and it was business as usual at the *Broadway Times.*

It was nearing four o'clock when the phone on the battered roll-top desk rang. Bart answered and said, "Hardin speaking."

The same monotonic voice of the night before said, "You should stay home, Hardin. We been calling. Did Santa Claus come to see you?"

Bart said, "He arrived on schedule. Thanks for the present. I'll be going to the theatre tomorrow evening."

The voice said, "That's all I wanted to know. You won't hear from us again if you're a good boy. We'll do our part. You do yours."

"I'm always a good boy at Christmas time," Bart answered.

The voice laughed unpleasantly and rang off.

By four o'clock the main rush of the day was over. At this hour Bart usually walked down to the Sligo Slasher's for his first drink of the day. But today he had something else to do during the break. He examined his wallet, clucked his tongue when he discovered how small a cash reserve he had. He took a twenty from the wallet, stuffing it into his trousers' pocket. He donned his coat and hat and left the building. The rain had stopped but a mist hung like dirty smoke over the churned slush of the almost deserted street. Twilight was early on this gloomy day and lighted signs had already begun to shimmer in the city's fog.

Across the street in a lunchroom a tall, seedy-looking man with a prominent Adam's apple, and a plump man in a burberry coat, sat on stools by the window, drinking coffee.

The seedy-looking man spoke suddenly, whispering, "That's him that just come out."

The plump man in the burberry said, "You're sure?"

"Listen, mister," the seedy-looking man answered. "I been on Jacobs Beach for twenty years. I know all the characters. That's Hardin. I hope he ain't in no trouble, though. He's a right guy that will always stake you to a flop and crackers when the good things lose."

The man in the burberry slid off the stool, paid his check, still looking intently out the window. He said, "Don't worry. Just keep your mouth shut. That's all you've got to do." He handed the seedy man a bill and left the lunchroom unobtrusively. He did not cross the street, but as Hardin headed downtown, he headed downtown, too.

In front of the Garden entrance Bart encountered a heavily built old Negro who was wearing a tattered sweater as a shield against the cold, wet wind. His name was Tom Trigg and years before he had been a great heavyweight. Bart said, "Tom, I told you I had that old overcoat of my dad's for you. I took it to the office yesterday. You want to catch pneumonia? Why didn't you come around and pick it up?"

The old man said, "I was around, Mist' Bart. I come up there noontime, like you said, but you wasn't in. I thought you was taking Christmas off."

"Come on," said Bart. "We'll go back and get it."

As they turned back toward Fifty-first, Bart noticed that this usually bustling corner was virtually deserted. There was only one person to be seen across the street. He was a plump man who wore a burberry. He had been walking south, but he seemed suddenly to change his mind, stood uncertainly for a minute, then turned his back and examined the display in a drug-store window.

Bart led old Tom Trigg to his office, took a dark blue chesterfield with a velvet collar from the clothes tree. His father had had formal taste. "Try it on," Bart said.

The old heavyweight struggled into the garment. It was a bit tight across the chest, but it would do.

"Man," said Trigg, with a yellow-toothed grin, "this is real fancy. If I was forty-seven years younger, the Sweet Georgia Browns would really dig me in this set of threads."

Bart said, "Don't you hock it, Tom, or swap it for a fifth of gin."

"Like gin mighty well," Tom answered as they left the building. "Gin's an old man's friend. But gin ain't got no fancy velvet collar on it."

Bart noted with surprise that the plump man in the burberry had moved up the street and was loitering in the cold. When he bid good-bye to Trigg in front of the Garden, Hardin glanced covertly over his shoulder. The plump man was still across the street, walking down-town again at a slow, casual pace.

Old Tom said, "Thanks a millyum for the threads, Mist' Bart. Only trouble with 'em is I look so prosperous I can't brace no handouts from the sports."

Bart grinned, slipped the old man a bill. "Here's enough for Christmas dinner, anyway," he said. "Get yourself some turkey."

Trigg cackled with laughter. "Turkey with juniper sauce," he said. "Ain't nothing like it for an old man like me."

Hardin walked to Forty-sixth and turned west. As he neared Ninth Avenue he paused to light a cigarette, stole another glance over his shoulder. The plump man in the burberry was still across the street, some fifty feet behind

76

him. Bart's brow creased in puzzlement. He went up the stoop of a brownstone that was in the tertiary stages of decay. In a window of the parlor floor was a crudely lettered sign on a shirt board. It read: "Rooms. Rates to the Profession."

The disheveled landlady who answered Bart's ring had been in vaudeville on the Pantages wheel once. She greeted Bart warmly, told him she was sure James Lennox was in his room. She had just taken him a turkey leg and a piece of pumpkin pie. "Poor old man," she said. "All alone on Christmas. I asked him to come down and eat with us in the kitchen, but he's got his pride, I guess. Claimed he had an engagement, but I know the only place he's got to go is that beanery on the corner."

Lennox was an aging, unemployed actor who had been a friend of Bart's father. He was a small and delicate little man with long white hair that curled over the frayed but scrupulously clean collar of his shirt. For years now he had lived on home relief and on stakes that Bart gave him in the guise of payment for stories about the old days on Broadway that Lennox occasionally wrote for the *Broadway Times*. Since Slade's business office refused to pay for such space copy, Bart had bought the stories out of his own pocket. Lennox's eyes were bright and there was a childlike sweetness in his old face.

Lennox said, "Bart! It was good of you to give up your time to pay me a Christmas visit."

Hardin encountered so little gratitude on Broadway that expressions of appreciation always embarrassed him. He answered, more curtly than he intended, "I had to see you on a business matter. But first I want you to do something for me. Will you pull down that window shade and turn off the light? I'm not making like the villain in a melodrama. There's a reason."

Lennox looked at Bart wide-eyed for a moment, then he said, "Why, of course, of course." He switched off the dim bulb that was burning in the lamp beside his cot, lowered the cracked green window shade. Hardin went to the window, pulled the shade back an inch and peered out. The plump man in the burberry was standing in the doorway of a plumbing establishment that was closed and darkened. Hardin's main reaction was one of annoyance. He had planned to ask James Lennox to have Christmas dinner with him at the Saddle and Whip, but if he was being followed he could not involve the innocent old man in his affairs.

He took the twenty-dollar bill he had removed from the dwindling capital in his wallet, put it on the table, switched on the lamp. He grinned at Lennox and said, "I guess I've got the jitters. I thought someone was following me. But I was wrong. This is a little Christmas bonus for you from the office. It's not much. Nobody got much this year."

Lennox said, "But, Bart, I'm not a regular employee. I don't think I'm entitled to this."

Bart said, "If Maddox Slade gives you something, you're entitled to it. I came about something else, too. Something personal. I want you to do me a favor."

"Why, of course, Bart. Anything at all."

78

"I want you to attend a play tomorrow night," Bart went on.

"But, Bart! I love the theatre. It's been my life. It's you who is doing me the favor."

Bart said, "It won't be too good a production, I'm afraid. It's a presentation of *Camino Réal*, at an off-Broadway house down in the Village. Opportunity, Incorporated, it's called."

Lennox nodded. "I've heard of them," he said. "It will be a pleasure. I've read the Williams play. It's wonderful. But I never had a chance to see it performed."

"I'm coming to you because you're about the only person on Broadway who can be completely trusted," Bart told the old man. "I'm afraid I can't tell you the reason for all this. You'll just have to follow instructions and ask no questions. Some day I'll tell you what it's all about. Tomorrow, you go down to this house on Bleecker Street and buy yourself a ticket for the night's performance. Tell the man you're far-sighted or something and want a seat in the rear. I'll be sitting in Row L, Seat 102. When I come in, don't recognize me. I'll put a brief case under the seat. When the lights dim at the end of Scene 2, I'll get up and walk out, leaving the brief case. I think somebody is going to pick it up. Your job is to get a look at the person who picks it up and to describe him as accurately as possible. I think you'd better stay for the entire performance, so you won't attract attention by leaving early. When it's over, meet me at the Sligo Slasher's bar on Forty-ninth, just across from the Garden, and tell me all about it."

The old man looked puzzled, but he nodded his head. He said, "I'll follow instructions, Bart. Is that all you want me to do?"

Bart took a ten from his pocket. His finances were now alarmingly low, but he laid the bill beside the twenty and said, "You'll need money for the ticket."

"But it won't cost that much, Bart. Besides, I have the bonus money. I can buy my own ticket. That's the least I could do after all the help you've given me."

"I had intended to take you out for Christmas dinner," Bart told the old man, "but something has come up. Buy yourself a turkey dinner on me."

As Hardin was leaving, Lennox called after him timidly, "Bart . . ."

Bart turned toward the old actor. "Bart, the landlady just brought me up a turkey leg. I ate it because I was feeling rather weak and peaked. But I really don't like turkey much. Would it be all right if I had steak instead?"

Bart grinned and said, "Sure. You have the biggest steak on Broadway."

The plump man was still waiting across the street when Bart left the rooming house. Hardin barely glanced at him.

Bart stopped off at the Sligo Slasher's for one quick double Irish on his way back to the office. For the next two hours he busied himself with making up the paper. At a little after seven the old firehouse shook as the presses began to roll.

Hardin scribbled a few corrections on a sample copy, sent it to the copy-cutter in the composing room and called it a day. The plump and patient man in the burberry was across the street, shivering in the cold. Hardin led him to the Saddle and Whip, where he spent nearly two hours over dinner, drinks and two good cigars. Before he left the restaurant, he went into a phone booth and dialed Manhattan West. When Romano came on the line, he said, "I want to ask you one straight question, Copper. Have you got a tail on me?"

Romano was silent for a moment, then he said, "Well, it's kind of a silly question. If I had a tail on you I'd have to lie about it because I'm a cop. Cops are awful liars sometimes. But the truth is, I haven't got a tail on you. I didn't even think about it. Maybe I was what they call derelict in my duty, because if I put a tail on you, I might find Slade and I want to talk to Slade. But the way I figure it, that Hodgson might have told the truth and Slade might be out of town and it can't hurt too much if we wait until tomorrow night before we see him."

"Thanks," Bart said. "It's a funny thing, but I almost always believe what you tell me. Maybe I'm just a sucker for Homicide Lieutenants."

He hung up and left the Saddle and Whip. Broadway looked as if it were on fire. Its lights glowed like flame behind a blanket of smoky fog that was rolling in from the ocean and the rivers now.

The plump man in the burberry had not risked waiting too far away because of the state of visibility. He was not more than a dozen feet from the door of the Saddle and Whip.

As Hardin's feet churned through the slush toward

Forty-second Street, he thought, the man could be one of the kidnappers, of course. But he knew he wasn't. Oh, well, he thought. I guess it's only natural Slade should take precautions. I've got his draft for fifty grand in my pocket and he thinks I've also got his ever-loving wife.

Hardin turned west toward the flea circus at Forty-second. Just before he reached his door, he about-faced suddenly. His shadow was caught off-guard. He ducked around, pretended to look into a window. Bart took a cigarette from his pocket, walked slowly toward the man in the burberry. He tapped the plump man on the shoulder and said, "Got a light, chum?"

The plump man shook his head, not looking at Bart, his face still averted. He tried to move off.

Bart held to his arm. He said, "Peeping's a hell of a way to earn your cornflakes, especially on Christmas, isn't it? It's tough weather, too. There's a gin mill across the street. If you sit on the end stool you can drink and watch my door if the fog's not too bad. But it's a waste of time. I'm not going out again. Have your agency tell Slade his boy went home at nine o'clock tonight."

Bart released his grip on the plump man, laughed and said, "Merry Christmas, chum."

He turned in the door to the flea circus and went upstairs.

Since there was nothing better to do, he turned on the television set. As usual, Betty Furness was jumping out of an oven into a refrigerator.

six

The plump man in the burberry was not waiting when Hardin left his flat at the unusally early hour of eight-thirty on the morning after Christmas, but a tall man in a blue coat, a gray homburg and horn-rimmed glasses was stationed in a doorway across the street. Hardin did not spot the new tail at once. He was far more expert at his business than the other private detective. Hardin saw him first when he peered out the window of the Copper Skillet where he always ate his breakfast, although he seldom ate it at such an hour as this. Hardin's breakfasts were usually noonday meals. He was not sure of the man even then. He wasn't sure until he reached the Brokers Bank on Fifth Avenue near Forty-fifth.

The Brokers Bank was one of the oldest and soundest financial institutions in the country. Evidently its directors believed that a mid-Victorian setting was the best evidence of the bank's stability. The building itself was brownstone with Gothic adornments and the furnishings were heavy and time-scarred. Bart noted that potted plants appeared to be an important feature of the décor. The bank clerks, all well past middle age, worked behind fretwork cages that had marble counters. A dark, full-length oil portrait of the bank's first president, a man who resembled U. S. Grant both in beard and dress, glowered down upon the customers from the walls of a balcony reached by carpeted stairs.

Mr. Gerald Swayne, the president, was the only officer of the bank who had a private office. The other executives worked in a maze of railed-in enclosures. A beefy, uniformed guard and two severe-looking female secretaries who appeared to be well over sixty, looked suspiciously at Bart's fancy vest before he was finally admitted to Swayne's presence.

The furnishings of Swayne's office were as old-fashioned and downright shoddy as the rest of the institution. But Shayne himself was neither old-fashioned nor shoddy. He was a brisk, middle-aged man with graying hair and keen eyes and he was impeccably tailored. He had a small, thick, salt-speckled mustache and he had a habit of fingering it reflectively. When Bart produced the draft and his credentials, Swayne said, "Yes. This seems to be quite in order. I came down much earlier than usual because of Maddox—Mr. Slade, that is. He called. But you will have a short wait, I'm afraid. Yesterday was a bank holiday. Producing such a sum in small bills requires some—some routine."

He fingered the mustache, eyed Bart and said, "This is a most unusual request, really. If it were anyone but Maddox, Mr. Slade, it would almost seem that it involved blackmail, or ransom money, or something, well—irregular. But of course, that's not my business, really. He has the money deposited and he has a right to have it in any form he wishes—pennies, even, I suppose."

Bart thought, you're a real smart detective, mister, but he said, "I wouldn't know. I'm just the errand boy."

The money was finally produced by two tellers who were followed by an armed guard. It was counted in front of Bart.

"How do you intend to transport this sum of money, Mr. Hardin?" Swayne inquired.

Bart set the imitation-alligator brief case on the desk. "In this," he answered. "I hope it fits."

"Oh, it will fit, all right," Swayne assured him. "People have an exaggerated idea of how much space a large sum of currency occupies, even in small bills." But he almost winced as he looked at the cheap plastic case. Obviously he did not consider it a proper container for such a respectable sum of money. He said, "I will have one of our guards conduct you to your destination, Mr. Hardin. That would be safest. He has a license to carry firearms."

Bart said quickly, "That won't be necessary. Mr. Slade has employed a private detective to accompany me. He's downstairs now."

Hardin was stuffing the money, which was neatly banded into thousand-dollar packages, into the brief case. It fit with room to spare.

Bart zipped the brief case, rose. "I'll take this right up to Mr. Slade," he said. "Thank you for your courtesy."

"Well . . ." said Swayne doubtfully. "I'd really feel much better about this if you'd let me send the guard."

Bart shook his head and left the office.

At the bottom of the stairs he smiled. The man with the horn-rimmed glasses was at a counter, fumbling with deposit blanks. Bart walked up to him and said in a low voice, I'm going uptown now. To the Thackeray Hotel on West One Hundred and Fourteenth Street. I'm going to take a cab. I'd ask you to ride with me, but I know that wouldn't be according to the book. If you have trouble finding a cab yourself, you know the address anyway."

The man mumbled something about a mistake. Bart grinned and left the bank, with fifty thousand dollars in an imitation-leather brief case tucked snugly under his arm. It's against the law for taxis to cruise on Fifth Avenue. Bart hailed a westbound cab on Forty-fifth.

When he reached the Thackeray Hotel, Bart paid off the driver, his eyes searching the street for another cab. None appeared immediately. Hardin went inside the hotel entrance and stood by the door. Presently a cab pulled to the curbing down the street. Its passenger did not emerge at once. When the man with the horn-rimmed glasses finally stepped out to the sidewalk, Bart walked out of the hotel again. He put two fingers to his mouth and whistled shrilly. As the man's startled face turned toward him, Bart grinned and waved at him cheerily.

Still grinning, he re-entered the hotel and rode to the fourth floor on the rickety elevator.

Slade seemed oddly embarrassed when he opened the door to Hardin. The detective agency he employs must be an honest one, at least, Bart thought. They must have reported that their "subject" had discovered he was being followed.

Hardin set the stuffed brief case on the desk. He said, "There it is. We've got a lot of work to do listing these bills. There are twenty-five hundred of them altogether. I've told Pops Taylor I'll be late if I get in at all and he will cover me." Hardin took a rolled bundle of long gray copy paper and half a dozen sharpened pencils from his pockets. "I brought paper and pencil from the office," he said. "When Arlene is released you can have a stenographer cut stencils of the list and give copies to the police and newspapers. That will make the money too hot to hold. Or at least too hot to spend. It's the only way, since you refuse to call the police in now."

Slade said, "I repeat that I see no point at all in this. Getting Arlene back safely is all that matters."

"Don't you want to catch her kidnappers?" Bart asked.

Slade's narrowed eyes searched Hardin's face. "Do *you?*" he asked.

Bart said, "Yes. You may not believe it, but I don't like kidnappers."

Finally they set to work. Bart read off the serial numbers, thumbing through the thick packets of bills without removing the bandings. Slade copied down the numbers on the long sheets of copy paper. The maid knocked and asked to clean the room. Slade told her curtly not to return again until he had called the desk. He had opened the door only an inch or two. The maid could not see the small fortune in currency that Slade had piled upon the couch. She left, grumbling.

It took them nearly five hours to list and recheck the serial numbers. It was mid-afternoon when they were finally finished. Slade complained that his right hand was numb.

Hardin said, "I won't need the money before eight o'clock tonight. I'll leave it here with you till then."

"No, Hardin," Slade answered. "You take it. I'm making you entirely responsible in this matter."

"Where do you suggest I put it for safekeeping?" Hardin asked. "In the bottom drawer of my roll-top desk with the Irish bottle?"

Slade said, "There's a big safe in the business office. Have Hatcher, the business manager, put it there until you want it."

"The business office keeps civlized hours," Bart said. "Everybody who knows the combination to the safe knocks off work at five-thirty."

"Tell Hatcher to remain until you want the money."

"That will be a pleasure," Hardin said. "But Mr. Hatcher isn't going to like it. He's not like the boys in the city room. He punches clocks."

"Tell Mr. Hatcher that his orders come from me," said Slade, a little of his usual arrogance returning.

As Bart slipped into his coat, he said, "There's one other thing. Now that the critical time is getting close, I think you'd better call off your private peepers. They might make complications."

Slade flushed. He said, "I don't think I quite understand you, Hardin."

"Your private detectives," Hardin said flatly. "I haven't minded playing games with them up to now. I've rather enjoyed it, in fact. But if they follow me down to the Village tonight, the people who kidnapped your wife may see them and think they're cops. If that happens they may call the whole deal off."

"You think you're being followed?" Slade asked.

"Let's quit sparring," Hardin said. "I've got a few hours left to do the work you pay me for on the *Broadway Times*. The peeper last night was a chubby man in a burberry. The one today is tall and had a blue coat and horn-rimmed glasses. Peepers aren't as smart as they're supposed to be."

"If you are being followed, Hardin, it could be the police, or the kidnappers, even."

"It's not the cops," Hardin said. "And there's no point at all in the kidnappers exposing themselves like that, even if they are amateurs."

Slade regarded Hardin for a long while, his face inscrutable. Finally he said, "All right, Hardin. I employed an agency. It was for your own protection. You're a willful man. I didn't know what you might do. You were so insistent we should go to the police. If you did that on your own, I wanted to be forewarned. And you were going to have a great deal of money in your possession today. I thought it best you have a kind of bodyguard."

"Thanks," said Hardin. "The bank thought so, too. They offered to send one of their boys who packs a gun up here with me."

"No," Slade said. "It wouldn't have done to bring a bank employee up here."

Bart picked up the brief case. Slade called after him, "Hardin . . ."

Bart turned, faced Slade.

"Why did you go to that brownstone rooming house near Ninth Avenue yesterday?" Slade asked.

"To see the only honest man on Broadway," Bart answered.

He left the room and closed the door behind him.

He paid no attention to the blue-coated private operative who followed him to the office of the *Broadway Times*. He did not think a detective would be waiting when he left that evening. Slade's fear for Arlene's safety would prevent that, he felt sure.

Hatcher complained bitterly about remaining overtime to retrieve the brief case from the safe. Hardin enjoyed telling him it was the boss's orders. Constant cold war was waged between the business and editorial offices.

Hardin had been at his desk only a few minutes when his phone rang. It was James Lennox calling. The old man said, "I've been trying to get in touch with you, Bart. I wanted to tell you that you can't buy a ticket to that little theatre in the Village."

"You mean the house is sold out?" Bart asked, alarmed. He had depended heavily upon planting Lennox in the theatre.

"No," Lennox answered. "It's not that. It's just that they don't *sell* seats. They give them away. It seems they distribute complimentary vouchers in shops and restaurants and bars all over the Village. They can be exchanged at the box office for reserved seats on any night the person desires. They depend upon donations from the audience to pay their way."

"I see," said Bart. "Did you manage to get a seat?"

"Of course," Lennox answered. "They were very sur‍prised I wanted to *buy* a ticket, but they were glad enough to give me one even though I didn't have one of their complimentary vouchers. I managed to get one in the rear, too. It's in Row K. I think that's just in front of you, across the aisle. I should be able to see your seat clearly enough if I turn my head a bit when the time comes."

"Fine," said Bart. "And remember not to recognize me."

"I'll remember," Lennox promised. "And Bart, I had that steak. I went to the Saddle and Whip. It's the first time I've been inside the place since David Belasco gave a party a long, long time ago. You know what steak costs now, Bart? Five dollars!"

Bart chuckled and said, "I ate there myself. Sorry I missed you."

"I went early, Bart. Right after you left me. I hope no home-relief investigators saw me eating in an expen‍sive place like that. I might lose my little income."

Bart said, "Relief investigators don't eat in the Saddle and Whip. You're safe."

"Thank you, Bart," the old man said. "Thank you for giving me the most wonderful Christmas I've enjoyed in years."

Bart said, "See you tonight," and hung up. It was a fine world, he thought, when a piece of steak could mean a happy Christmas for an old man whose talents had en‍tertained thousands of theatre-goers over the years.

Hardin drummed his fingers on the desk, neglecting

the accumulation of work that was piling up in front of him. He was sure that his insistence on listing the serial numbers of the ransom bills had puzzled Slade. Slade believed that Bart was connected with this kidnapping scheme somehow, that he was going to share in the ransom money, and he could not understand why he would want to make it difficult to pass the twenties. Slade was wrong, insultingly and inexcusably wrong about that. But he might have been right about another matter. Slade had said he was a willful and stubborn man. Hardin had acted on his own in arranging to plant old Lennox in the theatre. He was about to act on his own again, without consulting Slade.

He picked up the phone, called Romano at Manhattan West. You could always find Romano on duty when a murder case was breaking. He was on duty now.

Hardin said, "I've been in touch with Slade. I can't tell you where he is, but I've got a proposition for you and I think you ought to take it. Slade will be home tonight, probably between nine and ten. I know you must have a man watching the house, waiting for him. If you try to talk to him tonight, you won't get anything. You won't get anything at all, I'm sure of that. You can bluster if you want to, and take him down to Manhattan West, but it won't do you one damned bit of good and you'll be asking for a mess of trouble later because Slade knows the top brass and calls the mayor by his first name. If you wait until tomorrow morning, you'll get his story and get it straight. You'll get even more than you expect,

I think. Maybe I'm talking out of turn but the advice I'm giving you is good and you should take it."

Romano said, "You must know quite a lot yourself to talk like that. Aren't we pals? Couldn't you give me just a little tip, maybe, honey boy?"

Bart said, "I've given you a tip. A damned good tip. Are you going to take it?"

Romano thought about it. He said at last, "Well, I can't see a few hours more will do much harm, now things have gone this far. This Drake will be just as dead tomorrow morning as he'll be tonight."

Bart said, with a certainty he did not feel, "I don't think you'll regret it."

"Maybe I'm a chump," Romano answered, "but I'll wait unless something pops to change my mind. By the way, the pixies still following you around?"

"They were this morning," Bart answered. "A big tall pixie who wore horn-rimmed glasses. But I think they've gone off-duty now."

"Words," said Romano. "You use more words and tell me less than any man I ever knew."

Bart said, "It's my newspaper training," and hung up.

Because of his late arrival, Bart did not take his usual tea-time break at the Sligo Slasher's. Instead, at four o'clock, he took his first drink of the day from the bottle in his drawer.

He worked steadily until the presses rolled at a few minutes after seven. After he had marked sample copies for correction, he donned his coat and hat and went back to the business office, a dimly lighted area at this hour of the evening. Hatcher was fuming as he got the brief case from the safe.

"What on earth's in this thing?" he asked. "It's heavy. I was supposed to attend a most important meeting of the Parent-Teachers Association in New Rochelle at eight o'clock tonight. I can't even get my train until after eight now."

Bart grinned and said, "We all have to make sacrifices for our beloved employer."

When he left the office, he spotted no one he thought might be an operative tailing him. He had decided to eat his dinner at an Italian restaurant in the Village, not far from the Opportunity, Incorporated Theatre. He took a cab to MacDougal Street.

MacDougal had always been a fascinating street to Hardin. For a brief part of its length it was called Washington Square West and it was lined by large, opulent apartment buildings with canopies and doormen. At West Fourth, where the dubiously Georgian New York University Law School stood incongruously, MacDougal suddenly resumed its own rowdy identity and became a street of age-grimed tenements mazed with fire escapes, tiny pre-revolutionary houses that seemed to lean in the wind, and innumerable gift shops, coffee shops and bars. Near Third was a soot-stained, sedate brick house with ironwork trellises. Here a gentle lady named Louisa May Alcott had written a book called *Little Women*.

Hardin stopped the cab at the corner of Minetta Lane, a dark and desolate little street with an inappropriately romantic name. He entered a bar and restaurant called the Minetta Tavern.

The front part of the Minetta was a bar and it was decorated by framed caricatures of the tavern's customers —and by many of the customers themselves. At the bar a bald and bug-eyed little artist was exhibiting a painting to a sardonic-looking man in rumpled tweeds. "Look at that color, man!" he exclaimed. "It glows! I've got it at last. It's the fifth dimension!"

"The fifth?" said the man in tweeds. "What happened to the fourth dimension? Did you skip that one?"

"The fourth!" said the artist contemptuously. "I went through *that* stage long ago!"

A tall man with a silky beard and a Christ-like face passed among the customers quietly hawking privately printed volumes of poetry.

The walls of the dining room in the rear were given over to softly painted murals of Greenwich Village scenes of another era, when Eugene O'Neill had swept café floors in payment for his meals and Edna St. Vincent Millay had burned her candle and her genius at both ends. The room was well filled, but Bart found a small table near the open kitchen where a mustachioed chef in an enormous cap was juggling flaming copper pans. A polite young waiter the other customers addressed as Ray attempted to relieve Bart of the brief case, but Hardin shook his head. He sat at the small table, holding the menu in his hands and squeezing fifty thousand dollars between his feet.

Ray recommended a specialty of the house, *osso buco,*

veal knuckle served with yellow rice and a spicy sauce, and Hardin ordered it. It would be a change from the steak or chops he ate almost every night on Broadway. Hardin observed the people about him. They seemed quiet and relaxed in contrast to the strained and harried denizens of the world of Broadway. These people were pleasantly concerned with their food and drink and they exchanged banter with an affable young man named Eddie who seemed to be the proprietor and who moved solicitously from table to table. The Village had a reputation for wildness and vice, but Bart suspected that was largely due to the uptown crowd that chose this area of the city for their Saturday night sinning. The Village was a good name for this section, he thought. People came here to find an oasis in the teeming city and to rediscover the simple values of small towns among the friendly neighborhood Italians.

Hardin finished his dinner with *zabaglione*, a custardy, wine-flavored dessert. He lingered over the strong Italian coffee, loath to leave this pleasant place and to walk back into his own world where the only values were represented by the printed paper in the plastic brief case that was squeezed between his feet.

Hardin glanced at his watch and saw he had a few minutes to spare before his appointment at the theatre on Bleecker Street. He stopped at the bar and had a drink of Irish and was idiotically pleased to learn that the pleasant, broad-faced man who served him gloried in the name of Romeo. "Lots of people call me Wat, though,"

Romeo confided. "W-A-T, get it? 'Wherefore art thou, Romeo?' "

Hardin left the restaurant and walked south on Mac-Dougal. He passed one of the numerous Village coffee shops. In front of it a group of painfully self-conscious young people dressed in blue jeans were discussing the relative importance of their Ids and their Super Egos. Hardin thought of the bald artist and the bearded poetry salesman. It's only the old and the young who dare to be eccentric, he reflected. In his middle years man always conforms to that great myth called The Normal.

Hardin turned east at Bleecker. This was a grimmer street, lacking the rather cheery, Harlequin quality of MacDougal. The drab aspect of this section was largely due to a prison-like building that advertised "Rooms 75 Cents—Men Only." The "men only" stood in little clusters on the street despite the cold, drinking furtively from bottles. They were a shabby and defeated and hopeless lot. Next door to an automatic laundry was a grimy store that advertised "Rare Books Bought and Sold, Hours 9 p.m. to Midnight." Nice working hours if you can get them, Bart thought.

He finally came on the Opportunity, Incorporated Theatre, which sported a canopy and a large sign. Next door was a store window that bore the legend "Weird Things, Inc., Carberry Payne, Prop." Romano had mentioned the theatrical producer's other enterprise. Hardin glanced at his watch. He had three minutes to kill if he was to enter the theatre exactly at eight-forty as he had been instructed. He paused and looked into the shop window. Payne's merchandise was as weird as advertised, judging from the window display. There were a rhinestone-studded fly swatter, a mink dog-collar and a gold-plated beer-can opener, among other items.

At eight-thirty-nine Hardin entered the theater. A bald man with a Vandyke beard and twinkling eyes took Bart's ticket. From Romano's description, Hardin guessed the man was Carberry Payne. He also guessed that the little theatre had once been a Village night club. The floor was level and the seats were straight chairs set in one wide center section and two narrow sections at the side. It could accommodate no more than one hundred and fifty people and it was no more than half-filled. The stage, covered now by heavy green draw curtains, seemed to be an afterthought. Bart handed his ticket stub to the girl usher. She was young and dark and very lovely. Her sloppy-joe sweater could not conceal the softly molded curves of her young body. Bart wondered if she was Violet Brent, the girl whom Detective Grierson had interviewed the day before. She looked at the ticket stub and said, "Why, you're 'way in back, mister." She waited expectantly as if she expected Bart to request her to change the location of his seat.

Bart said, "That's fine. I like to sit in back."

The girl said, "There's a checkroom if you want to leave your coat and brief case." Bart shook his head. The usher led him to an aisle seat on the left of the last row. Directly across the aisle, one row down, Bart could see the back of James Lennox's head. The old man turned as Bart seated himself, but there was no flicker of recognition on his actor's face. There were only three other people in the row where Bart was sitting. Two seats down was a thin, pale woman who wore an evening gown. Farther to the right was a heavily built and heavily bearded man dressed in rough tweeds and beside him was a small, gray-haired woman. No one was sitting directly in front of Bart.

Hardin removed his coat and put it on his lap beneath his hat. He placed the brief case carefully under the seat, making a little ceremony of it, in case they were watching him.

In a few minutes the house lights dimmed and the stage curtains parted.

It was almost pay-off time.

As the on-stage lights went up, the contrast between the set that the late Erik Drake had constructed for this production and the magnificent scenery designed by Lemuel Ayers for the original Broadway presentation was painfully apparent. It was, of course, a grave mistake for any little theatre to attempt so ambitious a production as this play in the first place, Bart thought. Tennessee Williams had visualized the whole theatre as the setting of the fantasy, utilizing not only the stage itself, but runways, aisles and even boxes for the action of the play. The Opportunity, Incorporated producers were forced to work within the limited area of a small converted night club on a shallow and rudimentary stage.

Drake's sets for the vaguely Latin-American town square with its waterless fountain were painted in the same depressing tones of gray that he had used for his abstract canvas of the flying ducks. What was worse, the sets seemed so flimsy that they wobbled perilously each time an actor crossed the stage or brushed against them. This was especially true of the flat upstage which was supposed to be a stone wall with an archway leading to a desert waste Williams called *"Terra Incognita."*

Upstage right, to Hardin's left, there was a chalked inscription on the wall. It read KILROY IS COMING.

When Kilroy arrives, I depart, Bart thought, his heels squeezing against the brief case between his feet.

Carberry Payne, who was listed on the program as the play's director as well as its producer, had evidently chosen to use the original Broadway acting script and to eliminate the prologue that the playwright had written into a later version. The play began with Scene 1 of the first act. The scene was a very short one and in less than five minutes, the interlocutor, a character called Gutman, lit a cigar and declaimed "Block Two on the *Camino Réal!*" and the lights went down, although the curtain was not pulled across the stage.

Hardin frowned. Since the curtain was not drawn and characters had to make entrances and exits and rearrange themselves upon the stage before the second scene, the house was plunged into almost complete darkness. He wondered if Lennox would be able to see anything at all, even from so short a distance, at the end of the next scene, which was Bart's cue to leave. Fortunately the lights were down only a few instants. It would be a difficult task indeed for anyone to get to Hardin's seat, pick up the brief case and leave in that short space of time without Lennox detecting him.

The second scene was much longer than the first. It was after nine o'clock when Howard Barnaby, who played the role of Kilroy, made his entrance. It was quite an entrance, Bart thought. In the Broadway production, Eli Wallach, who had played the part of the prizefighter who

101

was dying because his "heart was as big as a baby's head," had brought an appealing quality of wistfulness to the characterization. He had stumbled through the archway that led to the desert wasteland, dust-caked, humble and bewildered. Barnaby seemed determined to play the role to the hilt, with all the histrionics of Junius Brutus Booth. He fairly stormed through the archway onto the steps leading to the stage and his entrance almost brought disaster. The flat of the stone wall shook violently and then began to lean forward at an acute angle. Barnaby was forced to grasp the tottering piece of scenery with his right hand to steady it and keep it from collapsing. A little ripple of laughter ran through the audience. It was almost time for Bart to leave, but he sat for a moment, studying Barnaby. He was a broad-shouldered, handsome young man with a full, sulky mouth and flashing dark eyes. As he held to the tottering scenery, he glared over the footlights at the audience, seeming to dare them to laugh at the mishap. Barnaby took a piece of chalk from his pocket and turned toward the inscription, KILROY IS COMING. He was still holding to the flat with one hand as he scratched out the word COMING and wrote in the word HERE.

The lights were beginning to go down. Bart rose, leaving the fifty thousand dollars in the brief case beneath his seat. On the way out he brushed against something soft and female and wondered it if was the pretty usher. The theatre was in almost complete darkness as he reached the exit and heard the actor playing Gutman cry, "Ho

102

ho!—a clown! The Eternal Punchinello! That's exactly what's needed in a crisis! Block Three on the *Camino Réal*."

There was a complete blackout as he pushed a door and went into the small, lighted lobby. Carberry Payne was in the lobby. He was arranging a series of large dinner plates upon a table. Above the table was a sign reading "Our Experiments in the Living Theatre Are Made Possible by the Generosity of Our Patrons. Please Leave Your Donation Here."

Payne looked up at Bart, surprise on his face. He said, "My goodness! I hope we aren't that bad! Are you leaving already?"

Bart averted his head, mumbled something about needing air. He was out on the street before he realized he had left no contribution for the support of the living theatre. That was out of character. Hardin considered himself the softest touch on Broadway. Oh, well, he thought wryly, I guess I left a pretty big contribution, at that. Fifty thousand dollars.

Hardin found a drugstore on a corner a block from the theatre. He went into a phone booth and dialed the number of the Thackeray Hotel. When Slade came on the wire, Bart said, "I left the package in the proper place about five minutes ago, according to instructions. If they keep their word, you should see the person you expect within an hour, sometime between ten and eleven. The person I mention will doubtless go to your home. Perhaps you'd better be there when they arrive."

Slade was silent a moment, then he said, "The—I mean, there may be people I don't wish to see waiting there for me."

"I can promise you no one is going to bother you tonight," Bart told him. "I can promise that because I'm a willful man, like you said, and I took action on my own. I talked to our friend, Romano. He's going to wait until tomorrow before he calls on you. By that time there'll be no reason to stall them further. Either the person you expect will have been home for hours or we will know the worst. In either case we'll need Romano's help by then."

Slade said, "All right. I'll have to take your word. I'll leave here at once."

Bart gave Slade the number of the Sligo Slasher's bar. He asked him to call him there when the person they expected appeared.

Hardin flagged a cab and rode uptown to Tony Maclaren's establishment on Jacobs Beach, across from the Garden. He took his Irish slowly despite Maclaren's frequent proddings to have another on the house. He didn't want too much of an edge tonight. He had things to do. He was determined upon taking more action on his own as soon as he had Lennox's report and knew Arlene's fate.

An hour passed and there was no call from Slade. Bart waited. He thought of calling Slade, but he decided it was useless. He would wait for Lennox.

It was eleven-thirty when the old actor finally appeared. His old-fashioned garb and his childishly innocent face were ludicrously incongruous here among the sports writers and fight managers and Jacobs Beach hangers-on who patronized the Sligo Slasher's bar.

Lennox appeared to be bursting with news, but Bart silenced him with a shake of his head, asked him what he wanted to drink. Lennox asked for a glass of port. Bart ordered it, had his own glass refilled with Irish. He picked up the drinks and led Lennox to a small room in back. There were a few tables with soiled, checked cloths in the room. The room was almost never used. Maclaren's customers liked to drink and argue at the bar. Maclaren called this cubbyhole his "conference room."

Lennox and Bart seated themselves at one of the tables. The old man said, "Bart, I was afraid I'd failed you. The house was in complete darkness for an incredible length of time after that second scene. I think it was because that young actor made too energetic an entrance and almost knocked the backdrop over. Evidently they were trying to right the scenery, to prop it, in the dark instead of just pulling the curtain. You could hear them doing it on the stage. I didn't want to attract attention to myself, but I leaned out in the aisle as far as I could and strained my eyes, trying to accustom them to the darkness, but I'm really afraid I couldn't actually see the seat you had occupied. Then there was a crash on the stage. Evidently one of the flats had collapsed completely while they were fooling with it. They pulled the curtain then and put the house lights up. I was greatly relieved. No one had taken your brief case. It was still right there under the seat where you had left it."

Astonishment showed on Bart's face. They had had an

almost perfect setup despite the precautions he had taken. "You say it was still there?" he asked.

Lennox nodded. "Yes, Bart. I watched it furtively all through the rest of the performance. Nobody took it. When the play was over I lingered on a few moments, getting into my overcoat. Maybe you noticed that heavy man with the thick black beard who sat a few seats down from you with a little gray-haired lady. He stumbled over the brief case on the way out. He picked it up and handed it to that usher, the young girl who was very pretty despite that most unbecoming sweat-shirt thing she wore. The little bald man with the beard—I assume he's the theatre manager—may have opened it when he took it into his office."

Hardin tapped his clutched fists softly on the table. His pale eyes looked beyond Lennox to a bad chromo of Man o' War that decorated the wall of the "conference room." He stared at the lithograph but he did not see it.

Lennox looked troubled. He said, "I'm afraid I've disappointed you, Bart. I'm afraid I haven't lived up to your expectations."

Bart said, "It's not that. You've done everything I could have possibly expected—more. But this business has taken a queer turn. I can't quite understand it. It's not your fault, though."

"Of course I have no idea at all what it's about," the old man said, "but if I can be of any further help . . ."

Bart shook his head. He fumbled in his pocket and said, "There's nothing else you can do right now. But I want to pay you for your trouble."

The old man smiled. "No, Bart. I won't take more money. It was a pleasure going to the theatre. It wasn't a very professional production, of course, but it did me good to see those young people, so intense, so eager. I won't take money from you, Bart. You've done enough for me already."

"If that's the way you feel, I won't offer it," Bart answered. "I have to make a phone call and then go down to the Village and pick up the brief case, if there's anyone left in the theatre."

Lennox rose, refused another glass of port. "Good night, Bart," he said. "I hope this works out, whatever it is. I can tell that you are troubled."

"It'll work out," Bart replied. "Everything works out one way or another. But sometimes the way it works out isn't nice."

He went to the phone booth, dialed the number of Slade's Gracie Square apartment. Hodgson had apparently returned from Staten Island. He answered the phone. Slade came on a moment later.

Slade's voice was cold. He said, "She hasn't come back, Hardin. I suppose you know that."

"They must have changed their plans without informing us," Bart said. "They didn't pick up the ransom."

He told Slade about Lennox, about what had happened in the theatre.

Slade said, "You disregarded my wishes completely in planting a man there in the theatre, if you are actually telling me the truth. They might have seen the man. That *might* have been the reason they did not pick up the satchel. But all that's beside the point now. I'm going to tell you something, Hardin. Please listen carefully."

When Slade spoke again his voice was hard, emotionless. It was the voice of a judge pronouncing sentence on a criminal. Slade said, "I have no interest in the money. It is only a means of getting my wife back. But if my wife is not returned to me unharmed I'm going to break you, Hardin. That's not a threat. It's a statement. I have some power. I will use all the power and all the money I have if necessary to break you. I won't hesitate to send you to prison if I can. Think about it, Hardin. I mean every word I say."

Bart waited until the flaming anger died before he spoke. He had regained control of himself and his voice was calm when he said, "I'm going down to the Village now to get your fifty thousand dollars. I'll bring it to you. If the kidnappers want to use me further in this business, I'll be available until your wife is safe. But I'm taking no orders from you from now on. I'm playing it my own way, no matter what happens."

"Are you going to the police, Hardin?" Slade asked. "I rather doubt you would do that now."

Bart said, "I'm not going to the police tonight. I'll give you your chance to tell Romano the truth when he calls on you tomorrow. If you don't tell him the truth, I will. The whole truth."

Slade said, "I think we have made our positions clear. I think we understand each other."

"Yes," Hardin answered, "I think we do."

eight

It was midnight when Hardin's cab pulled up in front of the Opportunity, Incorporated Theatre on Bleecker Street. The area was fairly deserted and the theatre was dark, but a man and a woman were standing in front of the box office, bundled up in coats and chatting in the loud and rather affected tones of theatrical people. As Bart walked toward them he recognized the red-haired woman as the actress who had played Lady Mulligan that evening and the man as the actor who had had the role of the debonair innkeeper, Gutman.

The man said, "When the flat started falling I thought it was going to hit me smack on the noggin and spoil one of my best sides."

The woman answered, "Wasn't it awful? Somebody should tell that boy he's not playing *Tarzan of the Apes.* I mean, he kind of *leaps.*"

Bart approached them and said, "Excuse me. Is Mr. Payne still inside?"

The red-haired woman shook her head. "He left a few minutes ago. But you can probably find him right next door. He runs that Weird Things shop. He lives in back."

Bart murmured thanks, turned to the shop next door. It was closed but a dim light was burning and the bald man with the Vandyke was visible inside. He seemed to be rearranging displays of his weird things. Bart tapped on the door. Payne's head swiveled toward the door and he stood uncertainly for a moment, shading his eyes, peering into the darkness. Then he walked to the door and opened it a crack on a safety chain. He said, "I'm afraid we're closed."

"I was at the theatre tonight. I left something. I thought it might have been turned in," Bart replied.

Payne scrutinized Bart. He said, "Oh, now I remember you. You're the man who was taken sick and had to get some air. You went rushing out during the first act, didn't you?"

"That's right."

Payne opened the door and said, "Come on in. Several things were turned in. People always lose things in theatres. You might not believe it, but we found a pair of women's high-heeled shoes once. Nobody ever called for them. The gal must have walked home in her stocking feet. And it was snowing that night, too."

He led Bart between counters on which his weird merchandise was piled, gestured toward a chair. "Sit a minute. I live in back. I've got the stuff that was turned in back there. What was it that you lost?" he said.

"A brief case," Bart answered. "A plastic case. It was imitation alligator."

Payne said, "Check. We've got it. It was turned in by a very famous man. You may have heard of him. Giorgio

Tresca, the sculptor. Big guy with a black beard. You might have noticed him. He must have been sitting in the same row with you. He's a good friend of ours. Attends all our productions and always leaves a twenty-buck donation. His stuff's in all the big galleries. Did that war memorial fountain down in Washington, you know. The one that kicked up all the controversy."

Bart didn't follow the art news very carefully but even he had heard of Tresca. He was world-famous. There seemed no possibility that such a man could be connected with a kidnapping scheme.

Payne said, "I'll get it. Want a drink? I was about to have a nightcap myself."

Bart doubted Payne had any Irish, but he agreed to the drink. He wanted a chance to talk to the man.

Payne went through some curtains that screened off the rear of the shop, returned with a bottle of rye, glasses and a water pitcher. He did not have the brief case. He said, "Important things first. Pour us a shot and I'll get the case. It's in back somewhere."

Bart poured whiskey, waited for Payne to return. The man with the Vandyke returned from the rear again, carrying the brief case. Bart's heart sank when he saw it. It was flat. His heart sank farther when Payne handed it to him and he felt its weight. He unzipped the brief case, looked inside. He said, "It's empty."

Payne looked at Bart suspiciously. "Sure, it's empty," he said. "It was empty when Tresca turned it in to Violet, the usher. It was empty when Violet handed it to me. It was still empty when I opened it back in my office."

111

"You looked inside?" Bart asked.

"Of course I looked inside. I always look inside something like a wallet or a handbag or a brief case when it's turned in. In the first place, there might be some identification of the owner. In the second place the contents might be valuable. If they are, I don't want to be responsible. I turn the article in to the police station."

Bart said, "There were valuable contents in this brief case when I left it in the theatre."

Payne's bright little eyes were slitted now and you could see the anger flooding slowly into his face. He said, "I don't like this, mister. I don't like it at all. What is this, a racket? I thought I knew them all."

"No racket," Bart answered. "There were valuable papers in this brief case."

Payne's face was thoroughly angry now. He said, "I think you'd better get out, mister. If it's a racket, you're wasting your time. Opportunity, Incorporated isn't a money-making enterprise. We barely manage to get by and pay expenses. You can't get anything from us with a nuisance suit. Get out, now, and take that piece of junk with you. Get out, or I'll call the cops."

Hardin made no pretense of being an acute judge of human nature. But for some reason he was convinced that this little man was righteously indignant and that he was telling the truth.

Bart said, "Maybe I'd better introduce myself. Since you're in the theatre you may possibly have heard of me. At least you know the paper I work for. I'm Hardin,

112

Bart Hardin of the *Broadway Times*." He opened his wallet, handed an identification card to Payne.

Payne said, in a different tone of voice, "Of course I've heard of you. You should have told me before I made an ass of myself. I wish I'd known you were coming down. I wish you could have stayed for more of the show, although we had a bad night with the scenery falling down and all. A little publicity in a Broadway sheet would do us a lot of good."

Bart said, "We'll talk about getting you some publicity. I like little theatre movements if they don't get too damned arty. The Broadway stage can benefit from them. But right now I'm interested in the brief case. It really did have valuable contents."

Payne tugged at his Vandyke, drank from his glass. He said, "Hardin, there's something damned screwy about this thing. I got a little shock when Violet handed it to me tonight. I couldn't think why, then I remembered. The last time I saw that case—or one just like it, since this is yours—it was being carried by a man who got himself murdered. Erik Drake, my scenic artist. But that's not all. There was something peculiar about this case that Drake was carrying, something that attracted my attention. I've racked my addled brain, but I can't think what the devil it was. It couldn't have been the *quality* of the thing. If you'll pardon my saying so, it's about as cheap an article as you can find."

Hardin said, "Please try to remember more about it. It's important. Vitally important to me."

Payne tugged at his beard again and said, "Hardin, I just can't. Not right now. It's been troubling me all evening. But if you'll give me a little time, it will come to me. I'm like that. I can't remember some pesky little fact and I stew about it and it does no good at all. Then I just store it in the back of my head and forget about it and it comes to me in my sleep or something. Anyway, it's there when I wake up in the morning. Almost always."

"You think this fact will be there tomorrow morning?"

Payne said, "I think it might be. It might be there when I wake up. Call me up or, better still, come down and see. But don't wake me up too early. I putter around all night, going over my stock or reading playscripts or something. I never get up before noon. If you asked me *anything* before noon, you wouldn't get a sensible answer. But there's something funny about that case, or about one just like it. I said so to Violet tonight when she handed it to me."

Bart said, "Tell me something about this Violet, your usher."

Payne was peering into the gloom toward the front of the shop. He said, "Wait a minute, Hardin. There's someone looking in the store window."

He walked toward the door of the shop, pressed his face against it. He returned in a moment and said, "Guess I'm seeing things. Or it was one of the winos from that flophouse across the street. You asked me about this Violet Brent. She's a stage-struck kid from the Midwest somewhere. All stage-struck kids are from the Midwest now-

114

adays, it seems. They used to come from the South, but they come from the Midwest now. Nice, sweet kid. She's nuts about that young bull Barnaby, who almost knocked my scenery down tonight. She's a nice kid and damned obliging. Ushers, fills in at the box office, plays small parts whenever she gets a chance. She hasn't had much chance yet, I'm afraid. She's understudy for Esmeralda, the Gypsy's daughter, in *Camino* but the other gal hasn't missed a night yet. She also understudied for the part of Laura Wingfield in another Williams play we gave, *The Glass Menagerie,* and she got on a time or two. Only regular part she's had was a character role. Played Martha Brewster, one of the crazy, murdering spinster sisters in Joe Kesselring's great comedy, *Arsenic and Old Lace.* But it had a short run. Came during the hot spell last summer and since the house isn't air-conditioned the customers stayed away in droves."

"She live near here?" Bart asked.

"That's right. Just around on Sullivan Street. Her papa sends her an allowance. Got a nice little garden studio. I'll give you the address if you want it. It would be a big break for her if you could give her a mention in the paper. You see, the way it is, I can't pay the kids anything. They even have to supply their own costumes if anything more than street clothes is required. What really happens is, I do pay them the Equity minimum for off-Broadway productions and they pay it right back to me for dramatic instruction. It's legitimate, an accepted system. That's the way nearly all the little theatres down here work. Equity's happy if you obey the letter of the law. The kids are happy to have a showcase for their talents and to get experience."

Hardin said, "I'd like to have Miss Brent's address. Could you write it down for me?"

"Sure," Payne answered. He took a business card of the Weird Things shop from a table, scribbled on the back of it with a ballpoint pen. Hardin made a mental note of the fact that Payne was right-handed.

Bart glanced at the card Payne handed him. "I suppose Miss Brent would be with her boy friend now," he said.

"You mean Barnaby? No. We have performances on Sundays and holidays and we're dark one weekday. Tomorrow's the day we're closed. Howard told me he was leaving right after the performance tonight to visit some friends in the country, Westchester or Long Island or somewhere, I think. He's got an old jalopy and he's driving out. But for God's sake don't go busting in on Violet at this hour of the night. You'd scare her to death. She fancies herself as an emancipated young woman, but she's still a kid and she was brought up in the Middle West. She wouldn't entertain a strange man in her apartment after midnight."

"I'd really like to ask her a few questions," Bart said. "But I guess they can wait. She was standing in back and she might possibly have seen someone open the brief case before it was turned in."

Payne shook his head vigorously, decisively. "No," he said. "If that had happened she'd have reported it to me when she handed in the article. There's not a chance of that. I can see you're very disturbed about this. Can you tell me what's missing from this case, Mr. Hardin?"

Hardin said, "Valuable papers. They belong to someone else. It's most embarrassing to me."

Payne scrutinized Hardin. "I can't quite understand this, I'm afraid," he said. "You came down here with a brief case full of valuable papers. You left the theatre before the performance was fairly under way and you were careless enough to leave the brief case beneath your seat. But it seems you didn't even miss it for hours, Hardin. At least you came down to recover it only a few minutes ago and you left the theatre a little after nine o'clock, I'd guess it was."

Bart thought of his hypochondriac friend Romano and his numerous symptoms. He said, "I ate oysters with my dinner. One of them must have been slightly tainted. I've—I've got what they call a nervous duodenal and my digestion's not too good. It began to hit me about the time the lights were going down on that second scene. I had to get some air. I was pretty sick for a while, too sick to think about anything but my stomach. When the spell was over I missed the brief case and came down here."

"A bum tummy can be a nasty thing, I guess," Payne answered. "Fortunately mine is made of cast iron. I'm fifty and the only medicine I ever take is B-12, the stay-young vitamin, they call it. But that's not what keeps me young. It's the theatre and the kids. Doing the work I like to do." His bright eyes regarded Hardin for a moment and he tugged reflectively at his little pointed beard. "I'll tell you something, Hardin, although I guess there's

117

really not much use, because it would be self-evident to you. There's only one person could possibly have removed those papers from your brief case."

"Who?" Hardin asked.

"Me, of course," said Payne disarmingly. "I'm the only possible suspect. Tresca picked that case up in full view of several persons, including myself. He didn't open it. He gave it to Violet. She handed it to me at once. It wasn't in her hands an instant, hardly. I took the case to my little office in the theatre and I opened it. If there were valuable contents, I'm the only one who could have removed them. It looks pretty black for me."

Hardin did not answer. The little man with the Vandyke beard lit a cigarette, blew smoke toward the ceiling. His eyes regarded Hardin and there was an expression of puzzled amusement in them. He said, "The circumstantial evidence is pretty strong, you see. You might even think it was stronger if you investigated my financial position. Providing those papers you say were in the case were negotiable, I might have been tempted, all right. I live rather happily from hand to mouth. I'm always in minor financial difficulties, it seems. Right now, because the shop did well during the Christmas season, I'm temporarily solvent, out of debt. But that's not always the case."

He blew more smoke, refilled the glasses from the whiskey bottle. "There are mitigating circumstances, though. You'll find things to balance the debit side of the ledger if you investigate me. The Manufacturers Bank doesn't ever bounce my checks and embarrass me. There's a nice guy there who knows me and he just calls up to say I'm a bit overdrawn and I should get it up. Banks have to trust you to do a thing like that and they don't trust many people. I can let the rent on the shop and the theatre run for several months if I need to without getting evicted and my credit in the neighborhood stores is practically unlimited. The Italians who own this section of town are pretty canny businessmen. They wouldn't be too likely to trust a thief."

The bearded man waited for Bart to speak. Hardin remained silent, sipping at his drink, watching Payne's face.

Payne said, "Since you have every reason to suspect me of stealing property that belongs to you, or property that you were trusted with, at least, I think I'll tell you something about myself. My story's a strange one, I suppose, and not too reassuring in the present instance. In my case, life really did begin at forty. That's when I came down here to the Village, just about ten years ago. Before that I was a broker and a pretty damned successful one. I had a good wife and two nice grown kids and a home on Long Island and a couple of cars and a motor launch. And I was plain bored to death. It was about that time I read a biography of Gauguin, the businessman who turned artist and left his family and went off to the South Seas. It did something to me. I suddenly realized I had an awful lot of money put by and that my business could be sold for a lot more. My kids were about to finish college. They didn't need me. My wife didn't, either. I was just a habit with her. So I turned all my money and all my property over to my wife and kids, enough to support them

119

comfortably for the rest of their lives. I kept five thousand dollars. That was the exact amount of money my dad had given me to start life when I left college. I thought I had that much coming to me for all those dreary years in a broker's office. I'd always been interested in the theatre, but I'd only been able to participate as a sixth-row-center first nighter in the past. I came down here to the Village and opened up my own theatre, and ran it the way I wanted to. Sometimes I produced plays by unheard-of playwrights that nobody else would produce. Sometimes I revived successful plays and gave ambitious kids a chance to act in them."

Payne drank, grinned at Bart. "Sounds like I'm a screwball, doesn't it?" he said. "Maybe I am. Maybe screwballs are the only really happy people in our fouled-up world. Anyway I'm happy. For the first time in my life. Did you ever see a happy man before, Hardin? They're curiosities nowadays, you know."

Hardin said, "I haven't seen very many, I'm afraid."

"No little theatre can pay its way," Payne went on. "I knew that. I knew I had to have a sideline. So I read another book. Books—two of them, anyway—have had a big influence on my life. This one was Thorstein Veblen and his theories of conspicuous waste. While I was reading it, it occurred to me that the only pleasures the big rich have which are denied to ordinary folks are the pleasures of conspicuous waste. At least that was the case before the present income taxes. I mean they put hideous diamond tiaras on their fat wives and installed enormous pipe organs in their homes and built marble mausoleums in Newport. I couldn't sell the middle classes tiaras and marble palaces and pipe organs at prices they could afford, but I could sell them things like jewel-studded fly swatters and real mink collars for their dogs and gold-plated beer-openers. So I opened this Weird Things, Incorporated shop. In my place the average person can enjoy the pleasures of conspicuous waste for the modest sum of about five bucks by purchasing something that's entirely frivolous and useless. The shop has helped support my hobby, the theatre, and it usually keeps me in three squares a day. I'm not interested in making money, just paying expenses. When a play I've produced by an unknown author gets on Broadway or when one of my kids gets a part with the Theatre Guild or goes to Hollywood, that's enough reward for me. That's the way I am, Hardin. You take me or you leave me, I guess."

Hardin said, "I think I'll take you."

Payne grinned, extended the bottle. "Thanks," he said. "Have another shot. You know, people think the Village is a place for young people with dreams in their heads. It is, in a way, but the kids mostly come here and sow a few oats and dream a few dreams, then go back to Iowa and work the rest of their lives in their papas' factories. Really the Village is a refuge for old codgers like me who don't like the way things are arranged in the other part of the world. I can't tell you what a kick I got out of growing this beard. I'd always wanted one, but a man with a beard would have been ostracized from Wall Street and the Saddle Rock Country Club. Down here the beard's just accepted as a part of my personality."

Hardin accepted another drink. "I guess a psychiatrist might make something out of these fancy vests I wear, too," he said. "I'm inclined to accept your own appraisal of yourself, without a psychoanalyst's report. It's an unenlightened viewpoint, I know, but all the psychoanalysts I've met have impressed me as having morbid minds. I accept your self-appraisal, but I'd still like to ask a few more questions."

Payne slumped back comfortably in his chair, savored his whiskey and said, "Shoot. The nicest part about being well adjusted is that even the most unusual things that happen to you are enjoyable. Cross-examine all you want."

The bearded man suddenly sat bolt upright in his chair, staring at the distant storefront. Then he rose and went to the display window. This time he moved very fast, almost running. He stood at the window a moment. Then he unlocked the door and went out into the dark street.

When he returned, Payne said, "There's no doubt about it this time. Someone *was* peering through that window. I couldn't get a good look at him, though. It must have been one of the winos from the flophouse, but I can't imagine one of them burglarizing the joint. What the hell would a bum like that do with a rhinestone-studded fly swatter? I haven't adapted my theories of conspicuous waste to quite that low an economic level. Sorry for the interruption, Hardin. Fire away."

Hardin said, "I'd like to ask if you remember anyone asking particularly for a seat in the back of the house for tonight's performance."

122

"Check," said Payne. "I remember someone doing just that. He was a little old man with long white hair and a remarkably angelic face."

Bart was disappointed. That would have been old James Lennox, of course. He said, "No one else?"

"I don't think so. Of course, Tresca and his wife always like to sit in the rear. They don't have to ask. They're regular customers and we put 'em there automatically. Also there's a skinny lady poet. She's got an Irish name, Casey, Riley, something like that. An old patron of ours. Makes her living doing research for one of the magazines. She always picks the last row so she can get out quick if she wants to. Claims she has spells, claustrophobia, and she wants to be near an exit."

Those were the only other people who had sat in the back row with Bart. He said, "You think the skinny lady-poet might have removed the contents and left the brief case under the seat?"

Payne shrugged. "From the little I know of her, it's not in character," he replied. "How bulky a package would the contents of the case have made?"

"Pretty bulky," Bart said.

"Then she didn't have it with her when she left," Payne declared. "We know our patrons pretty well, the regulars. We always watch for this gal especially, because she's kind of a standing joke with the staff, although I guess it's pathetic, really. She's the only customer who ever dresses formally for our productions. Invariably wears a green velvet evening dress and an opera cloak and carries a tiny beaded evening bag. I noticed she was dressed like that tonight and the little beaded bag was the only thing she was carrying when she left the theatre."

You couldn't carry fifty thousand dollars in twenty dollar bills in a little beaded evening bag, Bart thought.

"Tell me something about this scenic designer of yours who was murdered," Bart asked.

"Drake? You think there's some connection between his death and the loss of your property? I don't get the connection at all."

Bart said, "I don't either. It's just that there are two suspicious circumstances related to your theatre."

Payne nodded. "That's true enough. Frankly I didn't like Drake, or admire his work, either. He was a nasty, self-centered, carping little man. He lived with one of my actors, Howard Barnaby, for a while, but they fell out over the housekeeping arrangements or something and Howard moved. I wouldn't have chosen him as my scenic artist, but when it's for free, you can't be too particular. Drake had a stroke of luck just recently. Sold one of his paintings for a big price, I heard. Don't know how much. I heard Arlene Lash, Mrs. Maddox Slade, bought it. Say! Slade's owner of the sheet you work for, isn't he?"

Bart said, "That's right."

"Well, now! Maybe there *is* a connection. Did the stuff in the brief case belong to Slade or Slade's wife, maybe?"

Bart said, "I'm sorry but I can't tell you that. Not right now."

"Okay," said Payne. "Pardon me for asking. But Arlene's been a good friend of ours. She's interested in

124

young actors and she's given several of my kids a boost on Broadway. Also, she's brought a lot of Broadway big shots down to see our productions. She was very interested in Howard Barnaby. That's why I couldn't understand her buying the picture from Drake after Barnaby quarreled with him."

Bart said, "Do you think there was something between Arlene and Barnaby?"

"I try not to think about other people's private affairs," Payne answered. "I assume she was interested in him as an actor. She's been interested in several of my actors and helped them along." He grinned. "I admit most of them were young men with broad shoulders, but don't tell her husband I said that."

Bart rose and said, "Well, thanks for all the information. I'm sorry I had to make like a district attorney."

Payne extended his hand. "Thanks for not condemning me without a fair trial," he said. "I still say I'm the logical suspect. I'm terribly sorry about those missing papers. But there's something itching in the back of my head. Something about that brief case that was queer. It'll come to me."

"I hope it comes to you by noon tomorrow," Bart said. "I'll call you then, or drop down, maybe."

"Do that," Payne said. He walked to the front of the shop and unlocked the door.

Hardin started out. Then something on the counter near the door attracted his attention. It was a display of Christmas cards, seals, gift wrappings. One stack of paper was silver with a green abstract design that resembled fir

125

trees. It was exactly like the paper that had been wrapped around the brief case when Santa Claus delivered it on Christmas morning.

Hardin picked up a package of the paper and said, "This is most unusual. Where on earth did you find it?"

Payne said, "I'm afraid it's a bit too unusual. It was a design of Drake's. He persuaded a paper house down on Hudson to print up some of it for the Christmas season, and of course I had to stock a little. But hardly anybody bought it. Folks like the more conventional bells and holly wreaths at Christmastime, I guess. The modernists have never been too successful in attracting the Yuletide trade."

Hardin walked out into the night. He saw the glimmer of a neon bar sign across the street. He crossed and entered the bar. It was a dismal place and the customers were mostly the winos from the adjacent flophouse. But it had a phone booth. Bart dialed the Gracie Square number and this time Slade's voice answered.

Hardin said, "Is Arlene home yet?"

Slade's voice was flat and icy. He said, "Did you expect her to be? She isn't."

Bart waited a moment. Slade did not mention the ransom money. Hardin said, "I'm going to tell you something. There's not much point in telling it, I guess. But here it is. The brief case was turned in. It was turned in by a famous sculptor named Tresca and it's hard to believe he was involved in this. The case was empty."

There was silence on the line. Then Slade said, "So that's the story. All right, Hardin. I repeat that the money doesn't bother me. My wife had better get here tonight. That's what's important. Remember that, Hardin. And remember I meant every word I said to you when you called before. I can break you, Hardin, and I will."

Slade hung up the phone.

As Hardin pushed his way through the despondent wine-bibbers toward the door of the saloon, someone clutched his arm and said, "Hey, mister!"

Hardin turned, faced a beefy, red-faced man in dirty, tattered clothes. The man had been standing at the extreme end of the bar, almost against the window that looked out to the street. He blew a wino's sour breath into Hardin's face as he spoke. "Don't you remember me, mister? I thought it was you when you come in. Don't you remember Santa Claus, mister? I'm Old Fats. Melvin Holtzheimer."

Bart recognized the man now. He grinned and said, "What are you doing in the Village? I thought the Bowery was your beat."

Old Fats nodded. "It usually is," he answered, "but sometimes when the bracing's good and I'm in the chips I come here for a little change. There's a real swell pad next door, the Hill Hotel. They charge six bits a night but you get a private room and a locker and a washbowl."

"You're in the chips now?" Bart asked.

"Sure I am," Old Fats replied. "I made the touch with the widow lady and I made the touch with you and I turned in my uniform and collected my pay from the Volunteers. All on Christmas. So I'm living it up a little."

The bartender called to Bart, "Is that guy trying to pan-handle you, mister? It ain't allowed in here."

"He's a friend of mine," Bart answered.

Old Fats said, "Listen, mister. I've got something to tell you. You want to step outside a minute?"

Bart nodded, pushed the door open. They went out into the dark street. Another fog was rolling in from the Hudson now. The night air tasted like damp cotton-wool.

Old Fats said, "It's funny it was you."

"What do you mean?"

"You being followed, mister?"

"Why do you ask that?"

Hardin could see Old Fats' face in the red glow of the neon bar sign. It held a look of ludicrous cunning. The beefy man said, "There was a guy standing beside me in the bar tonight, right up against the window. He wasn't the kind of character belongs in a wino bar. Big guy, kind of young, with a gray hat and a pulled-up collar. I thought he was watching the theatre place across the street be-cause he kept staring out the window in that direction. But after a while, he went out and crossed the street and he didn't go to the theatre. He went to that electric shop next door and stuck his nose up against the window like he was trying to put the peek on the joint."

"Electric shop?" asked Bart.

"Sure. The one you just come out of. It's got a sign says 'Wired Things, Incorporated,' so I guess it's an electric shop."

Bart grinned and said, "Oh. Tell me more."

"Well he come back to the bar and he waited a while and then he went back and peeked through the window again and come back to the bar again. When you come out of the place, he ducked out of the bar like somebody had given him a hotfoot. I was looking out the window when you come out and I seen you come in here, but I didn't recognize you till you come out of the phone booth. So I thought I'd better tell you. If you own that electric shop, you better lock up good tonight. He could of been casing the joint for a heist."

"You didn't see where he went when I came out of the shop, did you?" Bart asked.

"He headed toward Thompson Street, walking fast. In this fog that's come up now, you couldn't see him if he was standing right next to us." The beefy man considered that possibility and there was alarm in his voice when he spoke again. "Why, maybe he *is!*" he said.

Bart said, "Maybe so. Anyway, you've earned yourself a few more days at the luxury hotel next door. Thanks, Melvin." He fished in his pocket, found a five and handed it to Old Fats.

"Mister," said Melvin, "I wish I met marks like you every day. I could have a nice old age."

Bart bid Old Fats good night. As he headed toward Sullivan Street he kept glancing over his shoulder, peer-

130

ing across the street. But he could see only a few feet in the rapidly gathering fog.

So Mr. Slade didn't call his peepers off, after all, he thought. Well, I don't envy the poor dope who's trying to tail me in this mess of weather. It was a ground fog that swirled around him, but it reached the second-story level of the buildings.

Old Fats stood uncertainly for a moment as Hardin disappeared into the smoky darkness. Wine had stimulated a sense of adventure in him. He crossed the street and walked toward the shop. A very dim light from the back of the shop was barely discernible through the fog. A man with a turned-up collar was tapping lightly on the door of the shop. Old Fats was almost upon the man before he saw him. The door opened and the man went in. Old Fats headed rapidly in the direction Hardin had taken. When he reached Sullivan Street, the edge of his bloodhound instincts was dulled. He couldn't see anything in the fog and he wanted a drink. He returned to the bar and ordered a double muscatel.

Hardin had turned left on Sullivan, heading south toward Houston. He paused several times and lit matches in the swirling gloom to examine house numbers. Finally he came to a row of solid, respectable-looking rose-brick buildings with white trim and found the number he was seeking. He walked into an outside foyer. In the dim light of the foyer, he examined his wrist watch. It was a quarter to one. It was hardly a proper hour to call on a strange young woman, even in Greenwich Village. But Hardin

131

found a bell marked Violet Brent and pressed it. He pressed it several times before the buzzer on the heavy door announced the lock had been released. He shoved the door and walked into a well-lighted, neat corridor. Scenic wallpaper in the corridor depicted green weeping-willow trees. Apartment 2 was at the extreme end of the corridor. The door was enameled a bright red and bore a brass numeral. It was closed. Bart tapped on it.

The door opened inches, revealing a small, impudently tilted nose and one eye fringed by long dark lashes. The girl's voice sounded sleepy. She said, "Howard? I thought you'd gone to the country hours ago."

Bart said, "It isn't Howard, but don't be frightened. Mr. Payne sent me. I left something in the theatre tonight."

The door opened more inches. Two eyes were now revealed. The eyes regarded Hardin. They traveled down, centered on the floral vest beneath his open trench coat. Violet Brent said, "I remember you. Mainly because of that gone vest you're wearing. You're the man who sat in the last row, aren't you? The one who left before the first act was over?"

Bart said, "That's right."

"I think you're the one who left the brief case," the girl said. "I turned it in to Carby, Mr. Payne. Didn't he give it to you?"

"He gave it to me," Hardin answered. "But the contents were missing. He thought you might give me some information."

The girl said, "Something was missing, you say? But *I*

132

wouldn't know anything about that. Carby was standing right beside me when Mr. Tresca handed the brief case in. I only had it in my hand a second. I took it and handed it to Carby. That was all."

"Mr. Payne told me that. But it would be helpful if I could ask you a couple of questions. Can't I come in for a minute?"

The girl hesitated, holding onto the door, her eyes searching Bart's face. Finally she said, "Oh, all right. But it's pretty late. You can only stay a minute. And don't get any ideas, mister."

She opened the door, turned her back on Bart and walked to the far end of the one-room studio apartment. She wore a quilted pink robe with ribbons and rosebuds at the neck and she looked even more teen-age in this garment than she had in the sloppy-joe sweater she had worn for her ushering job. The apartment was sparsely but neatly furnished with modern wrought-iron stuff. The studio bed was made with sheets and blankets and the covers were rumpled and the pillow dented, as if she had just risen from the couch. The small Christmas tree the girl and Barnaby had decorated stood on a low table, sparkling with ornaments and tinsel.

The girl paid no attention to Bart. She leaned down beside a radiator at the far end of the apartment as Hardin took a chair by a glass-topped coffee table that held ceramic ashtrays and a shadowy, theatrical photograph of Howard Barnaby. The girl picked up a heavy hammer. She sat in a small canvas sling chair beside the radiator, holding the hammer in her hand.

Bart grinned and said, "You going to hit me with that, honey?"

"No," Violet Brent answered seriously. "I don't intend to hit you. I'm going to hit the radiator, though, if you try anything funny. The superintendent sleeps just the other side of the wall and it makes a big noise if I hit the radiator with the hammer. He's a husky young Italian. The neighborhood hoodlums have been climbing into the garden recently, the nasty little Peeping Toms. So the super and I have arranged a signal."

Bart smiled at the embattled young woman in the quilted robe. "I accept the terms of the armed truce," he said. "My business isn't funny. It's pretty serious to me. My name's Hardin, Bart Hardin, and I'm managing editor of the *Broadway Times,* in case that helps to reassure you."

The girl said, "I suppose you came down here at one o'clock in the morning to put my picture in the paper. Please don't use the old talent-scout approach. That line's grown positively dreary."

"I've put pictures of kids who weren't half as pretty as you are in the paper," Bart told her. "But that's not what I'm here about. The contents of the brief case were valuable. I want them back."

"You think I've got whatever it is?" the girl asked. "I haven't, mister."

"I don't know who has the stuff," Bart said. "Payne said the case was empty when you handed it to him. He says you took nothing from it. The contents must have been removed during the performance and the case left under the seat. I thought perhaps you could tell me if you saw anyone fooling with the case before it was handed in. You were standing right back of the place where I was sitting, part of the time, at least."

"The first time I saw the case was when Mr. Tresca stumbled over it and picked it up and handed it to me," the girl answered. "I handed it to Carby Payne and that's all I know about it."

"Did it feel heavy while you had it in your hand?"

"No. It was quite light, in fact."

Bart said, "There's one other thing. Payne told me you help out sometimes at the box office. Do you recall anyone asking particularly for a seat in the back of the house for last night's performance?"

Violet Brent's brow wrinkled as she thought about it. Then she said, "Why, yes, I do! This person bought the ticket on Christmas Eve, I'm pretty sure of that. I remember they asked particularly for an end seat in the last row. Wait a minute! You know, I think I sold them a reservation for the very seat you occupied! Row L, Seat 102. Wasn't that your seat?"

Bart nodded. "Do you remember what this person looked like?"

"Yes. I remember, because the person was kind of a weirdy."

"In what way?"

Violet bit her full lower lip with small white teeth, concentrating on the memory before she said, "It was a little old lady in mourning clothes and she had a thick black veil. I remember that quite clearly now. I even

135

noticed something else. She was crippled. Not badly crippled, but I noticed she limped when she walked away from the box office."

"Did you know her? Had you ever seen her before?"

"No," the girl answered decisively. "I know a lot of our regular patrons by sight or name, but I'd never seen this one before. I'm quite sure of that."

Bart rose, said, "Thanks a lot. You've been of more help than you realize, maybe. Put your hammer away and get back to bed. Kids like you need a lot of sleep. I'm leaving." He walked to the door.

The girl rose. She still had the hammer in her hand. She looked at it, frowned and dropped it on a chair.

She said, "I guess I looked pretty silly with the hammer. But so many nasty things happen to girls who live alone nowadays."

Bart grinned at her. "Drop by the office sometime," he said. "Bring that picture along with you. A glossy print. If you can give us something to hang a caption on, we might use it."

The girl smiled and said, "You know, you're a nice guy in a funny kind of way. I'm almost sorry you didn't give me any cause to tap that radiator. It's not too flattering that you didn't, really."

Bart said, "Bring the photo up to the office. There won't be any pay-off."

He left the room and closed the door behind him.

The fog had become a huge gray specter in the darkness. Across the street, in front of Jimmy Kelly's night club,

136

boisterous voices were calling a cab. You could hear the revelers, but you could not see them.

Hardin turned left at Bleecker. When he reached a comparatively deserted stretch of the fog-bound street, he paused, listening for footsteps behind him. He paused and listened several times. He heard nothing in the muffled darkness. Slade's detective must have lost him in this ghostly mist, he thought.

It was after one o'clock. He had had little sleep in the past couple of days, but he had no thought of sleeping. The galling bitterness he felt against Slade and his suspicions, suspicions that now amounted almost to outright accusations, was like adrenalin. As he walked toward Sixth Avenue, his fists kept clenching and unclenching. He wanted to smash him. I'm reacting in the same way as a hopped-up hood, he told himself. Besides, you couldn't smash a man of Slade's age. And even if you did, nothing would be altered.

At this hour, his only alternatives were to go to bed or get drunk. He decided to get drunk. He finally found a cab on Sixth, parked near the subway station at West Third Street. He told the driver to take him to Forty-ninth and Eighth.

It was a long, slow trip through the fog-shrouded night. Bart paid the driver and started to head west on Jacobs Beach. Then he changed his mind, crossed Eighth Avenue again and walked to a bleak hostelry called the Buckingham Chambers. It was almost as depressing in its aspect as the men-only hotel on Bleecker Street, but old Pops

Taylor, the turf editor of the *Broadway Times,* had resided here ever since his wife had died.

The night clerk was a shirt-sleeved man with a face that belonged in a rogues' gallery. He was reading a copy of a tabloid newspaper and he barely looked up as Bart asked him if Pops was in his room. Pops would either be in his room, Bart knew, or he would be in a game. Old Pops Taylor lived for gambling.

The clerk finally deigned to look up at Bart. He said, "Pops? Maybe he's upstairs. We got modern conveniences in this pad. Why don't you try the house phone and find out?"

Bart picked up the phone. Old Pops was home. Bart said he was coming up.

Hardin grinned when he found the old man engrossed in a volume of *Scarne on Cards.*

Pops said, "You know, it's a damned shame that Moe Selig won't operate a faro bank in this town. According to these tables, the player's got more percentage in his favor bucking Old Tige than he has in any other card game. Maybe that's why Moe don't operate a bank."

"Maybe it's a neglected business opportunity," Bart answered. "Maybe I'll start one up. I dropped by to tell you you're managing editor until further notice."

"That right?" the old man asked without much interest, still scanning his percentage tables and making pencil marks in the book. "You going on a binge?"

Bart said, "Maybe."

"Make it a good one," the old man advised. "The way

138

I figure it, after forty years on the *Broadway Times* I'm entitled to one binge a year in addition to my vacation. I always make it last a week. A week's just right. You drink for a week, you get sick enough to quit, but you don't get sick enough to see the lavender leopards."

Bart said, "I always see men with white hair, pink faces and black eyebrows."

"They're bad, too," old Pops agreed.

"That's all," Bart said. "Carry on, Editor."

"Sure," Pops answered, making marks with his pencil. "Have a real good time. And let me know if you open up that faro bank."

Bart left the Buckingham Chambers and walked through the fog to the Sligo Slasher's bar across Eighth Avenue.

Tony Maclaren extended him the greeting he reserved for his best friends, regardless of their race or religion. "Hell! ya Protestant bum," he said, reaching for the Irish bottle. "Ya've been missing yer four o'clock nourishment the past few days. Ya wanna die of malnutrition?"

"Double Irish," Bart ordered. "And don't let the glass stay empty. I've only got about two hours."

Hardin drank and listened to Maclaren's tales of his fistic prowess until the bar closed at four o'clock. His glass had stayed empty only long enough to allow refilling. He felt the liquor but he wasn't weaving as he walked through the fog to the flea circus on Forty-second Street.

Bart poured a big nightcap from the bottle in his room.

He drank it, stripped off his clothes, and went to bed. He went to sleep almost instantly.

But he didn't sleep for long.

It was shortly after six in the morning when he was awakened to a cascading thunder of sound.

People were pounding on the door. They were fairly raining heavy blows against the door, in fact.

Bart threw a seersucker robe over his nude body, went to the door and fumbled with the latch as he cried out, "Who the hell is it?"

"It's the cops, Editor. Open up," said a voice Bart recognized as Romano's.

Bart opened the door.

Romano was accompanied by the square-built, frozen-faced young first-grade detective named Grierson. The lieutenant said, "You sleep tight. Grierson was about to break the door down. He's young and he gets impatient."

The two detectives walked past Bart.

Romano said, "Where were you around about midnight or a little later, Editor?"

Bart said, "Why?"

"Because I'm a cop and cops ask questions. This time I want an answer. Not double-talk."

"I was down in Greenwich Village talking to a man named Carberry Payne around that time," Bart answered. There was no use stalling. He knew Romano well enough to realize he was deadly serious.

Romano said, "That's too bad."

"Why?" asked Bart. "Why should it be?"

"Because a man named Carberry Payne has got himself murdered," Romano answered. "According to the medical examiner, he got himself murdered just about the time that you were with him."

ten

Bart's mind was still befuddled by whiskey and sleep. He said, "You mean Payne is dead?"

"People usually are when they get murdered," Romano answered.

Bart sat down heavily in a chair. He had liked the little man with the Vandyke beard. Payne had possessed moral courage few men could boast. He had traded wealth and the outward tokens of respectability for the kind of contentment that he wanted. "Did you ever see a happy man before?" Payne had asked. At least he died happy, Bart thought grimly. Maybe that was something. There had been something in the back of Payne's head, something that he could not quite recall, something about the brief case. He had seemed sure he would recall the elusive memory by noon. But he hadn't lived till noon. Someone had known he had knowledge of the brief case and had killed him because of it. Suddenly Bart remembered another thing that Payne had said. He'd said that it couldn't have been the *quality* of the brief case that had attracted his attention when he had seen it before. The remark had

had no significance to Hardin at the time. Now he thought it might have been very significant indeed.

Hardin's mind was still working slowly. The after-taste of whiskey was foul in his mouth and thin needles of pain were piercing into his temples. He said, "When was he killed?"

"Like I told you," Romano answered, "he was killed just about the time that you admit you were with him. The body was found a few minutes after three o'clock. It was found by a beat man from the Eighth Precinct. He makes a habit of trying the storekeepers' doors on his route to make sure they're locked. He knew Payne and was friendly with him. When he tried Payne's door it opened and he went in to try to wake Payne up, because he knew he lived in back. But he couldn't wake him up because he was dead on the floor of his shop, with a bullet hole in his back. Ballistics isn't through yet, but they think the same gun that killed Drake probably killed Payne."

Bart said, "He locked the door after me when I left around twelve-thirty, maybe a little later. He was very careful about it because he thought someone had been peeping through the window at us while we were talking."

"It wasn't locked when the cop passed by around three. The M.E. claims Payne had been dead two to five hours. He didn't want to guess any closer. But we've nailed it down a lot closer than that. He died between midnight and a few minutes after one o'clock. He left the theatre a few minutes before midnight. A couple of actors from the theatre, the ones who talked to you and told you Payne

143

was in his shop, saw him open the door to you a couple of minutes after midnight. The girl you went to see on Sullivan Street called Payne up right after you left her. She was puzzled by your visit and she wanted to ask about you. She knew he stayed up all night, so she phoned the shop. That was right around one, give or take a couple of minutes, she says. Payne didn't answer the phone. He probably didn't answer it because he was already dead there on the floor."

Hardin said, "You must have had a man on me to know about my going down there to see Payne, about my visiting the girl. You told me I wasn't being tailed, so I thought it was one of Slade's peepers who was shadowing me."

"I didn't have a tail on you," Romano said. "We had the addresses of everybody connected with Opportunity, Incorporated because of the Drake kill. We interviewed everybody we could find and we found 'em all except this Barnaby who's out of town and won't be back until tonight. A couple of the actors were standing outside the theatre when you drove up. You asked for Payne and they told you where he was. The description tallied. Those vests you wear are kind of noticeable. You introduced yourself to the girl when you called on her a little before one o'clock. Slade says he called his gumshoes off yesterday afternoon. He was afraid he wouldn't get his wife back if he kept them on the job. He told us you called him sometime between midnight and one o'clock and told him you were down in the neighborhood of the theatre. What makes you think that you were followed?"

"I thought the man Payne saw through the window was one of Slade's peepers. Maybe I was wrong. Maybe he was the man who murdered Payne. If he was, Payne must have known him. He was getting skittish about the face at the window and he wouldn't have let anyone he didn't know into the shop."

Romano said, "Maybe. But I've got to warn you the story's not too good. The only person who could verify the story of the man at the window is stone-cold dead."

Hardin said, "You're wrong. I've got verification."

"Who?"

Bart grinned weakly and said, "Santa Claus."

"Oh," Romano said. "That witness will be kind of hard to subpoena. He's back at the North Pole by now unless his reindeer gave out of gas."

"This one isn't," Bart declared. "He's in a pad on Bleecker Street. He also calls himself Old Fats and Melvin Holtzheimer."

Bart lit a cigarette and put it out immediately. It tasted like singed rat fur soaked in garlic. He said, "I take it from what you say that you've seen Slade."

"That's right," Romano replied. "I don't like disturbing millionaires at four o'clock in the morning but I can do it if I have to. I was going to play along with you and let him have his breakfast before I started asking questions. But when the kill came up it canceled all agreements. He told me everything, I guess. He told me about his wife buying the picture of the ducks from Drake, about her getting kidnapped when you were supposed to be with her. You been in lots of wrong places at the wrong time recently, it seems. He told me you were the go-between in paying off the ransom, too."

"Have they returned his wife?" Bart asked.

Romano shook his head. "No. That's what makes it tougher. Tougher for you, I mean."

Bart said, "Why?"

"Slade didn't come right out and say it, but he hinted pretty strong that he thinks you're mixed up in this. He thinks you're mixed up in the kidnapping to the extent of extorting the ransom money, anyway. And he's willing to believe you're mixed up in the kills, because the kills are tied in with the kidnapping."

Bart said, "He's got a high opinion of his managing editor."

Romano wagged his head in agreement. "Yeah," he said. "That's why I'm taking you downtown."

"You're taking me in? You're booking me?"

"I've got to take you in for questioning. There's no charge. Not yet. It seems that Slade and the D.A., Broderick, play tiddly-winks or whatever the hell big shots do when they meet in their private clubs. Slade called Broderick and told him everything, and said he wanted this matter prosecuted to the fullest extent and so forth. So we got to put a show on."

Bart said, "I can answer questions right here."

Romano shrugged. "When the D.A.'s in it, you put a show on. It wouldn't look official here."

"We're going to the D.A.'s office?"

"Uh-uh. Not this early in the morning. Broderick's sending an assistant D.A. down to Homicide at Manhattan West. He's sending one of the young ones, I'm sorry to say. The ones just out of law school are always going to reform the town over night. This one's name is Saltus. He's got freckles and red hair and he works strictly according to the book."

Bart thought a minute, pressed fingers to his aching head. He said, "Did Slade tell you why he went to the shooting gallery the night Drake got killed?"

"He told me," Romano answered. "He told me confidentially that he'd been jealous and suspicious of his wife because she was so much younger than he was. He found a slip of paper on the floor saying something about the Fun Arcade at midnight and he thought it might be the memo of a date she had with some boy friend. Because of the address, he thought the boy friend might possibly be you."

"That's silly as hell," Hardin said. "I was in his apartment that evening. He asked me to go after his wife when she barged out on him. He knew I was with her. If he wanted to find her, he'd have come to my apartment. He wouldn't have snooped around a shooting gallery."

Romano sighed and shrugged his heavy shoulders. "All a cop knows is what people tell him," he replied.

"Did he give you those serials numbers of the ransom bills I listed?"

"Yeah. But only after I asked him if he'd listed 'em. He didn't seem too anxious for me to have 'em, for some reason or another. The list should be mimeographed by now. It can't make the morning rags but it should hit the afternoon editions. The wire services are sending the list

147

out all over the country. And it's going over the police teletype to distribution centers within three hundred miles of the city."

Bart tried another cigarette. It tasted even worse than the first one. He stubbed it out. "How did Slade explain my insisting on him listing those serial numbers and making the money too hot to hold if he thinks I'm the one who's got it?" he asked.

"He didn't bother to explain," the lieutenant replied. "I think that kind of puzzled him. I'm supposed to be asking you questions and you're the one who's asking me. Get your clothes on. This Saltus couldn't question you in a bathrobe. It's too informal."

Bart said, "I think I've got a right to call my lawyer."

"I guess you have. It's your telephone and I can't stop you using it. Not unless I cut the wires. Who's your lawyer?"

"Marty Land, the Broadway Mouth. It's going to put him on a spot, not to mention waking him up a long time before his breakfast. He's counsel for the *Broadway Times*. Also he's Slade's personal attorney. And he's a friend of mine."

Hardin picked up the phone, dialed the very private number of a phone Marty Land kept beside his bed for the benefit of favored clients who did their transgressing outside business hours. Land's sleep-husky voice answered after the phone had rung several times.

Bart said, "This is Bart Hardin. I seem to be in trouble. I need legal counsel."

"My God," Land said, "do you have to get in trouble

at six-thirty in the morning? Can't it wait for daylight? What is it?"

"Murder," Bart answered. "Murder and kidnapping, maybe. I'd better warn you. It's Slade's wife who was kidnapped and he seems to think I'm involved. He's put the D.A. on me. Maybe you don't want to handle it."

Land's clients were mostly the producers and actors and mobsters who made up the world of Broadway. He was too inured to surprises to waste time in exclamations. He said, "Slade doesn't have a monopoly on my services. They're available to anybody who's in trouble and can pay for them."

"I've got about ten bucks in my pocket," Bart said.

"You'll hit a horse or draw locked aces in a game of stud. Where are they taking you?"

"To Manhattan West. Homicide."

Land was silent for a moment, as if he were taking time to jot the information on a pad. He said, "You sure they aren't hiding you at some precinct in the East Bronx, aren't you? If they're trying that, I'll pull the blankets off a judge I know and get a writ."

"I don't think so. Romano's the one who's taking me in. He says an assistant D.A. named Saltus is going to question me at Manhattan West."

Marty Land said, "Romano's one cop who tells the truth. Saltus is an eager-beaver, but eager-beavers usually aren't very smart. Stall them all you can. I've put my shoes and socks on while I've been talking, but it will take a little while for me to get there and I want to be waiting when you arrive."

Bart said, "Thanks, Marty."

"Don't thank me. You're paying when you hit the horse or catch the backed-up aces. There'll be a little extra on the retainer for waking me up at this hour. I was on a party half the night."

Bart hung up the phone and said to Romano, "There may be some eggs and things in the kitchenette. Suppose I cook some breakfast before we go down?"

"No," Romano answered flatly. "I'm willing to give you a reasonable amount of time to get Land down to Twentieth Street, but we don't stop for breakfast. And don't stall too much dressing, either. This Saltus does it according to the book."

Bart started for the bedroom. Grierson had been hovering by the door as if he expected Hardin to dash out and was guarding it. Grierson said, nodding toward the bedroom, "Should I go in?"

"My God, no," Romano replied. "Don't do it by the book like Saltus. Hardin's not going to jump out the window or swallow poison."

Bart went to the bathroom and took a cold shower, lingering in it as long as he dared. After he had dried himself, he swallowed an Empirin compound tablet for his headache and a benzedrine pill for his hangover. Then he began to shave. He was half through shaving when the stolid Grierson pushed the bathroom door open. "The lieutenant says to hurry up," he said.

"I can't go down like this," Bart protested. "Saltus couldn't question a man with lather on his face."

150

He managed to kill half an hour altogether. Romano had taken off his shoes. It took another minute or two for him to squeeze his swollen feet back into them. They went downstairs and got into the police car that was waiting at the curb.

The fog had lifted. The sun was not fully risen yet but the patches of sky that could be seen between the towering buildings were bright and the snow clouds of the previous days had disappeared.

Manhattan West was on the western fringes of the Chelsea district, not far from the teeming stretches of sinister repute called Hell's Kitchen, an area that supplied Homicide West with a large part of its business. Bart grinned as he saw Marty Land's huge Cadillac, complete to uniformed chauffeur, parked directly in front of the police station.

Romano chuckled. "Marty got here," he said. "I figured that he would."

Land was standing in a relaxed pose in front of the high desk as they entered the building. He was a slender man in a well-tailored, pin-stripe suit, a gray homburg and a carefully adjusted bow tie. Bart wondered how on earth he could appear so fresh and fashionable at this hour of the morning. He knew Land kept an electric razor in his car for such emergencies and he was immaculately shaved. Even his small mustache appeared to be freshly waxed. A vicuña coat was draped carelessly over his arm.

"Why, hello, Hardin!" Land said genially. "Fancy meeting you in a place like this. You must be slumming. Greetings, Lieutenant."

Romano nodded and said to the desk sergeant, "Saltus get here yet?"

"He's waiting in your office, Lieutenant," the desk man answered.

"Saltus!" exclaimed Marty. "I must run up and speak to him. Haven't seen him since I beat him in that Elroy murder case. It's a shame Broderick sends his young assistants to court with such weak cases. Doesn't help a lawyer's reputation any."

They went upstairs to Romano's office, a cubbyhole with battered furniture and a green-shaded desk lamp. Grierson did not accompany them, but even so the place was crowded.

Saltus was a gawky man in his thirties. His face and neck and the back of his big hands were splattered by freckles that looked like rusted ten-cent pieces. He had a large nose with nostrils that quivered noticeably as he inhaled his breath. His red hair was barbered into the short spikes called a crew cut.

Saltus took the initiative immediately. "Is this man Hardin?" he asked, pointing a finger at Bart.

Romano grunted agreement. Saltus faced Land and said, "What are you doing here, Land?"

"Just came up to shake your hand, Mr. Saltus," Marty answered affably, extending his manicured hand and exhibiting large cuff links with a heraldic design. "Also, Mr. Hardin happens to be my client."

Saltus touched the lawyer's hand briefly with his big paw and said, "You can't stay here. We want to question Hardin privately."

"Of course, Mr. Saltus. Question all you want. In the presence of his lawyer."

"I said privately," Saltus snapped. "This isn't a misdemeanor, Land. It's murder."

Land tchk-tchked. "A serious business, Mr. Saltus. All the more reason he should have counsel present. You and I tried a murder case recently, didn't we?"

Saltus' freckled face flushed. He said, "Do I have to order you out of here, Land?"

"I hope not, Mr. Saltus," Land replied amiably. "It would be a grave mistake. Surely you wouldn't deprive my client of his rights?"

"I have a right to question him privately," the red-haired man said.

"Only if you charge him."

"You want to force me to book him?"

Land tchk-tchked again. "I hope it doesn't come to that," he said. "Really I do. If you charge him I will have to get Judge Barker out of bed to sign a writ. He's an old man and he needs his rest."

Saltus' wide nostrils were quivering with something more than inhalation now. He said, "Old Judge Barker signs too many writs."

"I realize you and the Judge are of opposite political faiths," Land said. "But his name is still good on writs. They haven't outlawed the Republican Party yet in New York County, Mr. Saltus."

There was silence in the room while Saltus glared at Land and Land smiled winningly at Saltus.

"Are you charging my client, Mr. Saltus?" Land asked.

"I'm not charging him—yet," Saltus answered.

"In that case I'll make myself comfortable, with your permission," Marty said. He hung his homburg and vicuña on a clothes tree, sat down in a straight chair. He draped an arm over the back of the chair, extended his long and handsomely covered legs, the picture of relaxed composure.

He smiled happily at Saltus, exhibiting white and even teeth. "You may inquire, Mr. District Attorney," he said. "My client has nothing to withhold."

For twenty minutes the red-haired district attorney questioned and Bart told him the same essential facts he had related to Romano earlier. During that period Land sat smiling and nodding occasionally and did not interrupt once. Finally, as Saltus paused to scrutinize the scribbled notes he had been making, Marty raised his hand. He said, "Mr. Saltus, I'm sure that your time as an energetic public servant is far more valuable than ours. I suggest that we are wasting it. There is a corroborative witness to Mr. Hardin's statement—the intriguing gentleman variously known as Santa Claus, Old Fats and Melvin Holtzheimer. He is known to be lodging temporarily in a men's hotel on Bleecker Street. He is obviously a vagrant and he may not be there long. I suggest we go down immediately and interview him while we can. I know something about these flophouses, as they're called. Tenants are not allowed to occupy their rooms after nine o'clock in the morning. From nine to four, they fumigate. I know this, because I have had to find witnesses in these places before. Once they're out of their

154

rooms, they're hard to find. It's almost eight. I suggest we adjourn to this men's hotel and interview the witness."

"Trustworthy witnesses you must have recruited from flophouses," said Saltus, a sneer in his voice.

"*All* my witnesses are trustworthy, Mr. Saltus," Land declared. "That's why I win so many cases. I always say it's the integrity of the witness, not the persuasiveness of the lawyer that counts most with a jury."

Saltus balked at going to the hotel on Bleecker Street. He demanded that the witness be picked up and brought to Manhattan West.

Land said, "More wasted time, Mr. Saltus. The man will not be registered under his own name. They never are. A detective or a uniformed policeman seeking to locate him would run up against a wall of silence. The only way to find him is to take down someone who knows him. Hardin is the only one of us who knows the man."

Finally Marty's arguments prevailed. The two lawyers, Romano and Hardin piled into Land's custom-built Cadillac and were driven the short distance to Bleecker by the uniformed chauffeur. A few of the bums from the hotel had already gathered on the street in front of the grim, gray structure. They looked curiously at the Cadillac and the men inside it as it pulled to the curbing.

The lobby of the hotel was tiled like the corridor of a hospital and it smelled of antiseptic like a hospital. Shabby tenants were already seated in the hard wooden armchairs of the lobby. As Hardin and the others entered, the seated men gave them a startled look, then averted their eyes and began to mumble to each other behind grimy hands. The clerk at the desk was a small man with a ferret's face. A short wino and a tall wino had just turned in their keys and were teetering against the desk, the dazed look of hangover on their unshaven faces. "Man, I got to promote a shot," the short wino was saying. "Man, I got the creeping sickness."

Saltus walked officially to the desk clerk, took identification from his pocket and extended it. "I'm from the district attorney's office," he announced. "I want the number of the room occupied by Melvin Holtzheimer."

Without looking at a register, the clerk said, as if it were an automatic answer, "We got no one of that name."

Land pushed himself in front of Saltus. "Of course, you haven't," he said, smiling ingratiatingly. "I promise you he's in no trouble. We just need a little information. This man is a good friend of his." He nodded toward Hardin. "Of course he wouldn't register under the name of Holtzheimer, but I'm sure you know him. A big, fat fellow, getting along in years. He was a Santa Claus for the Volunteers. Has a ruddy face and he's been here since Christmas."

"Old Fats!" exclaimed the short wino. "I know Old Fats! He and I was drinking together. *You* know Old Fats," he said to the room clerk.

The tall wino slapped the short wino across the face. "Shaddap you lousy, stinking stoolie," he said.

"Maybe I know him," the room clerk said, looking uncomfortable. "There's a guy in 409 looks something like

that." He sheafed through cards and said, "He's registered as John Jones."

"What an uninspired alias," commented Land. "Shall
we go to 409, gentlemen?"

Saltus was disgruntled and determined to assert his
authority. He said to the room clerk, "Come along with
us and bring a key in case we can't get in."

"I can't leave this desk!" the room clerk declared. "The
boy on the elevator's got a key if you want one."

The elevator was an open, enormous affair that resembled a freight lift and moved very slowly. They found
the cubicle marked 409 in one of the winding corridors of
the fourth floor and Saltus rapped smartly on the door.
He rapped smartly several times before it was opened.

Old Fats' ponderous belly bulged out of a suit of long
underwear when he opened the door. "What the hell, it's
nine o'clock already?" he asked, rubbing at gummed eyes.
When he saw his visitors, he exclaimed "What the hell?"
again. Saltus pushed a hand against the old man's chest
and forced his way into the room. Old Fats glared at Saltus. "You're Law!" he declared. "I can smell out Law
like a bird dog smells out feathers."

The old man discovered Bart and said, "Why it's you,
boss! I went running after you last night, but I lost you
in the fog. I wanted to tell you something. Right after
you left me I crossed the street to that shop the fellow
had been peeping in. And I almost run right into him!
He was standing there knocking on the door and somebody opened it and let him in."

"Well, Mr. Saltus," said Land, "does that tie it up for you?"

Saltus fumed and fussed and questioned. But in the end he could present no good reason for holding Hardin in the face of the old man's unsolicited statement which indicated Payne had been alive after Hardin left him. He warned Hardin and Melvin Holtzheimer not to leave the city and to be available whenever they were wanted for further questioning. Old Fats assured Saltus that if he couldn't be found at the Hill Hotel or the Castle Rooms or the Palace Bar and Grill, or the Bowery Mission, he could always be located through the Sally Ann. Land grinned and told Saltus the Sally Ann meant the Salvation Army.

Land dropped Saltus and Romano off at Twentieth Street and drove Hardin to the Flea Circus. Bart climbed the steps of his apartment, stripped off his clothes and went to bed. He was just pulling up the covers when the phone rang.

When Hardin heard Romano's voice, he said, "Oh, no! Not again!"

Romano said, "There was something I forgot to tell you. Maybe I shouldn't have told you, anyway, while you were a murder suspect. They found a twenty-dollar bill beside Payne's body. I asked 'em to check the serial number against that list Slade gave me, just on an off-chance. It was one of the ransom bills."

"That's very interesting," Bart said.

"Yeah," Romano answered. "There's one other thing. I'm pretty sure this Saltus is going to make a stake-out

158

at your flat with cops from the D.A.'s office. If you murder anybody else, you'd better shake the guy who's tailing you first."

Bart said, "After I get a little sleep I'll lead him to some very cultural places. I'm going to an art school and a book store."

Hardin went to bed again. He set his alarm clock for noon. He would get three hours' sleep, anyway. It was just nine o'clock.

eleven

The bell tower of Yale University was chiming nine when a well-dressed woman with a black eye walked into a police station in New Haven, Connecticut.

The desk sergeant was a fatherly-looking man with a kind face and iron-gray hair. He did not see the woman immediately. He was busy listening to a young man in a hound's-tooth jacket who was explaining that he'd gone on a party the night before and parked his car somewhere, he couldn't just remember the exact location, and that he couldn't find it. He said he was particularly anxious to find the car as it had been a Christmas present from his father. He described it as a sports car, a white Jaguar with gold trim.

The desk sergeant said, "We found your car, all right. It was parked at an angle the wrong way of a one-way street right up against a fire plug. As soon as we get through writing out violations for you, we'll tell you where it is."

The sergeant discovered the well-dressed woman and looked curiously at her blackened eye. He said, "What's *your* trouble, ma'am?"

The woman said, "It sounds crazy."

The sergeant waited. You were used to crazy things when you worked in a police station in a college town.

The woman said, "I seem to have lost my memory. I don't know who I am."

"Tell me all about it," the sergeant suggested gently. He looked at her black eye again and said, "Were you in an accident?"

"Why do you ask that?" the woman said.

"Because you've got a shiner, ma'am. A black eye."

She raised her hand to her face, touched the bruised area and said, "Ouch. It hurts when I touch it."

"What's the last thing you remember, ma'am?"

"It was just a few minutes ago, as if I were suddenly coming out of a deep sleep. I was walking along a street and I was cold. The street wasn't familiar to me. Suddenly I realized *nothing* was familiar. I didn't even know my name."

The sergeant nodded. Amnesia was an old story to any cop.

"An elderly man was passing by," the woman continued. "I stopped him and asked him where I was. He told me the name of the street, but that didn't mean anything to me. I asked him what town I was in. He said I was in New Haven. I have no idea how I got here. I don't seem to *belong* here, somehow or other. But I don't know where I belong."

The young man in the hound's-tooth jacket was staring at the woman with absorbed interest. He smiled secretively.

The sergeant said, "Let me see your pocketbook, ma'am. There might be identification."

She handed him a large leather bag. The sergeant opened it and said, "There's nothing inside but a lipstick, a compact, a little comb and a twenty-dollar bill. No identification."

The young man in the hound's-tooth jacket spoke suddenly, eagerly. "*I* can tell you who you are, lady," he said. "You're Arlene Lash, the actress. Only now you're Mrs. Maddox Slade."

The woman with the black eye turned toward him. "Really?" she asked. "Do I know you?"

"No," the Yale student answered. "But I've been drooling at you from the third row center for years now. And your husband and my father are friends. They both belong to the Criterion Club. Maybe I'd better introduce myself. I'm Gerald Swayne, Jr. and my father's president of the Brokers Trust. You may know him socially. I think he's visited in your place on Gracie Square."

The woman said, "Those names seem to ring a tiny little bell, but I'm still pretty confused. I'm afraid I still don't remember much."

A detective had come out from a room in the rear. He had been observing the proceedings with boredom up to now. Sudden interest and a look of alacrity came into his face. He crossed to the desk and said to the young man, "You say this lady's name is Mrs. Maddox Slade? You're sure?"

The young man nodded and said, "Certain-sure."

The detective turned to the gray-haired desk sergeant.

He said, "A squeal came in from New York quite a while ago. Mrs. Maddox Slade was kidnapped. She's been missing since Christmas Eve." He looked at the woman and said, "The fur coat checks with the description of the clothes she was wearing when she disappeared."

He looked at the articles from the leather bag, picked up the twenty-dollar bill and said, "Let me have this a minute. A list of the ransom bills just came through in distribution from Bridgeport."

The detective walked back to the rear room. The sergeant climbed down from his little platform, held a swinging gate open and said to the woman, "Please come back here, ma'am, and take a chair. I'm going to call a police doctor. You may have other injuries besides that eye. We'll call your husband in New York right away." He turned to the young man. "Gracie Square, you said?" he asked.

The young man nodded vigorously.

The detective was in the rear room for several minutes. When he returned, he said, "It checks all right. This is one of the ransom bills."

The young man in the hound's-tooth jacket grinned at the sergeant. "I've been a big help to the police," he declared. "Why can't you just forget about those violations?"

The sergeant regarded the young man benignly. "Because I'm not a forgetful man," he answered, as he began to fill out the traffic violation tickets.

twelve

Hardin didn't get to sleep three hours after all. The alarm clock didn't ring before noon, but the telephone did. It rang about a quarter of twelve.

Romano said, "I thought maybe you'd like to know they've found Mrs. Slade. They found her up in New Haven. She's been walking around with a hard case of amnesia, it seems, and she's got a black eye and she had one of the ransom bills in her pocketbook."

Bart said, "I'm glad they found her alive. I'm surprised, too."

"Slade arranged to charter a plane and to have her brought to New York in care of a trained nurse through some banker friend of his who's got a son at Yale," Romano continued. "He's just checked her in at the Sutton Hospital. It's one of those private places on the East Side. They won't admit you unless you've got some fashionable disease like a nervous breakdown or acute alcoholism. She can't remember anything. The medics tell me that if a person with amnesia sees somebody directly connected with the thing that caused them to lose their memory, they may come out of shock and start remembering. You must have been the last person she saw before she was snatched. I want her to see you as soon as possible. I'll be out in front of your house in exactly fifteen minutes with a car. I'm going to drive you to the hospital."

"Slade won't like my seeing his wife," Bart said.

"No," Romano answered. "He won't. He'll forbid it, in fact. But you're going in to see her just the same."

Bart hurried into his clothes. His hangover had disappeared and he was hungry. He knew he'd have no time to eat at the Copper Skillet. He broke two raw eggs into a glass of tomato juice, spiked it with Worcestershire sauce and drank that. He had time for one cup of instant coffee. The forgotten alarm clock began to whirr at twelve o'clock. Bart switched it off and went downstairs. Romano was already waiting at the curb in an old black Buick driven by Grierson.

The hospital was far east, almost to the river. It was a graystone building that resembled an elegant town house more than an infirmary. Only a small and decorous brass plate on the door identified it as a hospital.

Grierson remained in the car. Romano and Hardin took an elevator to the top floor of the building which resembled an exclusive club inside. They were stopped by a starched and severe floor nurse whose desk blocked a passageway to the private rooms on the floor. She would not allow them to pass, despite Romano's badge, until she had called Maddox Slade.

Slade glared at Hardin and said to Romano, "Why did you bring Hardin? He can have no possible business here. The doctor does not wish my wife disturbed. She has been through a harrowing experience. She has re-covered her memory. That is to say, she knows her iden-tity and she recognized me and others. She remembers everything right up to the time she was kidnapped, but her mind has blacked that experience out. The doctor says it is a defense mechanism. I am willing to let you go in alone for just a few minutes, Lieutenant. But I will not allow Hardin in my wife's room."

Romano said, "Hardin goes in, too, Mr. Slade. If she sees him it may help her to remember what happened after she left his apartment on Christmas Eve."

"No!" Slade said. "I positively forbid it. If you take Hardin into her room, Lieutenant, I warn you that I will lodge a most vigorous protest with the authorities."

Romano sighed. "You know the mayor," he answered, "and you know the commissioner and you know the D.A. It happens I'm the one who's in charge of this case and I say Hardin goes in. Come on, Hardin."

Romano took Hardin by the arm, pushed him past Slade. Slade's face was scarlet with rage.

They found Arlene's room. It was enormous. It wasn't furnished with the standard white metal equipment of a hospital. There was scenic wallpaper and linen drapes and a hooked rug and Provincial style pieces and com-fortable chairs.

Romano nodded to the woman with the black eye. He said, "I'm a police officer, Mrs. Slade. I'm trying to find out what happened to you. Do you know this man who's with me?"

"Why, of course I know him," Arlene answered. "He's

166

Bart Hardin, managing editor of my husband's paper. Everything is coming back to me. I haven't quite lost my mind, it seems. Only what happened the past few days— Maddox says I was kidnapped—all that is a perfect blank."

"Do you remember being in my apartment?" Bart asked her.

She nodded. "I remember that. That's about the last thing I *do* remember. Why did you leave me there alone that night, Hardin?"

Hardin said, "I had to go out a few minutes and you were asleep. What happened after I left?"

"Liquor always makes me drowsy," Arlene declared. "I woke up and I was all alone and I guess I was a little irritated. I found my wrap and put it on and walked out into the hallway and started down the stairs. And that's the very last thing I can remember. I think someone must have been waiting, must have hit me on the head or drugged me or something. Anyway the next thing I knew I was walking down some street in New Haven, Connecticut and I had a black eye and it was almost three days later."

Bart said, "Did you see this artist, Drake, that night?"

She shook her head. "I'm pretty sure I didn't. Not before I walked out of that apartment, anyway."

"You had some appointment in the shooting gallery downstairs. Do you think you went down there?"

"I didn't go under my own power. At least I didn't go in my right mind. All I know is I stepped out of your apartment and everything blacked out."

Slade had been standing in the doorway, glowering at Romano and Hardin. He said, "All right, Lieutenant. You forced your way in here against my wishes and against the doctor's orders. If you stay a moment longer I'm going to call the resident physician."

Romano said, "I guess there's not much use in staying any longer. All I've found out is that she doesn't know anything. That's all I usually find out from witnesses, even the ones who don't have amnesia. Come on, Hardin."

Romano walked toward the door and Hardin followed him. As Hardin came abreast of Slade, he said, "Could you step outside a minute? I'd like to talk to you privately."

Slade said, "I've nothing to say to you, Hardin."

"It's pretty important," Hardin replied. "There's a little lounge across the hall. We can go in there. It won't take long. All you have to say is one of two words. And each word is one syllable."

Slade stood still for a moment, hate in his face as he stared at Hardin. Then without a word he walked out of the room and crossed the hallway to the little lounge.

Slade did not seat himself. He turned to Hardin and said, "What are these simple words you wish me to say?"

"I want you to answer a question," Hardin replied. "The answer is 'Yes' or it's 'No.' The question is, Will you pay five thousand dollars' reward if I recover your fifty thousand dollars ransom money?"

Slade's mouth twisted into a sneer. "So that's it! The afternoon papers are printing the serial numbers and the money's too hot to hold. So you're selling out cheap. A dime on the dollar."

"Just yes or no," said Hardin.

Slade said, "I've got my wife back and I don't care about the money. I told you that. But I suppose there's really no use in throwing such a sum away. I'll buy it back at that price, yes. Bring it to me and I'll write you a check for five thousand."

Hardin said, "That's all I wanted to know." He walked out of the room and rejoined Romano who was standing by the elevator, talking to Marty Land, the lawyer, who had apparently just arrived. Land took hold of Hardin's arm, drew him aside. "Don't worry about catching those backed-up aces to pay my fee for this morning's services," he said.

"Why?" Hardin asked.

"Because Slade has just called me in. He wants me to 'stand by to protect his interests,' whatever that means. I'll add your fee to his bill in a way he'll never notice."

Bart grinned and said, "I expect you'd add it whether I paid or not."

Marty chuckled. "You know," he said, "I rather think I would, at that."

Grierson was waiting in the Buick when they reached the street, but Romano did not get in immediately. He stood fumbling with a cigarette and matches, looking around him covertly. He said, "With this nervous stomach, I shouldn't smoke. I bought a book called *How to Stop Smoking*, but it didn't do me any good because I never got time to read it. Where you going, Hardin? We'll drop you off."

"I'm going to Greenwich Village," Bart answered. "I'll take a cab."

"Get in," Romano said. "I want to go down to that shop where Payne was murdered, anyway. We'll save you cab fare."

When they were seated in the car, the lieutenant said to Hardin, "In case you're interested, I think the D.A.'s men are in that gray Chevvy coupe. It's a hell of a situation when cops start tailing cops, isn't it?"

"This whole business is fouled up," Hardin replied. "When Arlene reappeared, it knocked a theory of mine all to pieces."

"Yeah," Romano replied casually. "I kind of figured that. You got any more theories?"

"Maybe," Hardin answered. "I'm working on one now. I'll let you know if anything comes of it."

"Do that," said Romano. "It's always nice to have private citizens co-operate with the authorities."

Bart asked Grierson to drop him at the corner of Fifth Avenue and Eighth Street. As he got out of the car, Romano said, "Well, anyway, they didn't kill her."

"No," Bart said. "Slade didn't kill her."

He walked west on Eighth Street.

Bart didn't bother looking for the gray Chevvy or the men inside it. If the D.A. wanted his cops to tail him, it was all right with Hardin. Cops had to earn their salaries doing something.

West Eighth ran for only one block, from Fifth to

Sixth. It was intersected at the south by the northern lim-
its of MacDougal. West Eighth was called the Main Street
of the Village. The Whitney Museum, which had been its
cultural center, had moved uptown. Gonfarone's famed
Italian Restaurant had been torn down long before
Hardin's day. At the corner of MacDougal was a land-
mark, the Jumble Shop, an old restaurant which now
flaunted a startlingly modernistic façade. The rest of the
street was devoted to art shops, picture-framers, stores
that sold lamps, women's sportswear and men's haberdashery that was mostly pink or fulvous yellow. There was
an arty picture show and strip-joint night clubs that appealed to the uptown trade and were never visited by
Village residents. There were numerous bars with a reputation of having a homosexual clientele, hamburger counters and drug stores. A few bookstores lent a measure of
dignity to the strident thoroughfare.

Bart thought he would find what he was looking for
here if he could find it anywhere. He found it halfway
down the block.

It was a weatherbeaten brick building with a high stoop
and a broken iron railing. In a window of the parlor
floor was displayed a large oil painting of an overly plump
nude. Beneath the painting was a hand-lettered sign:
BOHEMIA ART SCHOOL. LIFE CLASSES DAILY.

Bart walked up the steps with the broken railing and
entered a barren, musty hallway with bare wood floors.
He paused for a moment to accustom his eyes to the
gloom and a torrent of fur and sound hurled itself at him.
A small, black and loudly yelping Pomeranian dog was

171

attacking the cuff of his trousers. A man came running out of one of the rooms on the hallway. He was a round little man and he wore a paint-smeared lavender smock. The man picked up the snarling dog and said, "Now, now, Van Gogh! You mustn't bite the customers."

Holding the wriggling dog in his arms, he said to Bart, "We call him Van Gogh because he got one of his ears bitten off in a fight with a dachshund. You know the story of the great painter, Van Gogh, I suppose. He cut off his ear and gave it to a prostitute for a present."

"That was very thoughtful of him," Bart said.

The man said, "Do come into the office." He led the way into a large room, cluttered with canvases that were stacked against the wall. There was a desk in the room, an old chair that was oozing its hair-stuffing and several folding metal chairs. There was also an infant's play pen. The round man dropped the dog into the play pen and Van Gogh immediately began to register mournful protests in an ear-ripping treble.

"Van Gogh has the artistic temperament," the round man explained, raising his voice to be heard above the banshee wailing. "Now what is it we can do for you, sir?"

Bart said, "I am interested in taking up painting as a hobby. Like Ike and Winnie, you know. My doctor recommends it."

"There's no therapy to equal it, sir," the round man in the paint-smeared smock declared enthusiastically. "We begin a new term in just a couple of weeks, the second week in January. You must look over our little prospectus. If I can only find one."

172

He began to fumble through the litter of drawers in the desk and said, "I *know* we've got them somewhere. We have to hide everything from Van Gogh. He's so destructive. He ate a whole tube of cobalt blue once, but he has a marvelous digestion. It didn't seem to harm him in the least. He's always eating paint when he can get it. He must have Technicolored innards by now." ·

After he had plowed through the drawers, spilling papers on the floor, the round man sat for a moment pinching his lower lip in perplexity. Then he said happily, "I know where they are! They're in the safe!"

He crossed the room and opened the lid of a small, shiny garbage container. "We call this the safe," he explained, "because it's got a lid and Van Gogh can't get inside it."

He produced a sheaf of pamphlets and handed them to Bart. "There we are!" he said, as if he had accomplished a notable feat in finding them. Bart pretended to examine the advertising material. He said, "I wonder if I could look in on a class? Is one in progress now?"

The round man nodded. "I know you want to look in on a life class," he said. "All young men do. There's a model posing upstairs. Come along with me, please."

He led Bart up uncarpeted, rickety stairs and into a large, loftlike room. The room had a skylight, but it was so grimy the half a dozen students could not work by the north light it afforded. They were working under electricity. At the front of the studio was a small dais with a dusty green curtain behind it. A nude model was standing on the dais, her profile to the students who were working on canvasboard propped on small easels. She was overly plump, like the picture of the young woman in the window. Bart thought maybe it was the same girl. An instructor was moving about among the class. He said, "Let's fill in the background, please. Let's choose a background color before we begin to ripen up the flesh tints."

The students paid no attention to the dusty green curtain. Their backgrounds were variously yellows and reds and blues. Bart moved among them as they painted in the background, observing each carefully. Two of the students glared at him as he looked over their shoulders. They didn't seem to like kibitzers. Bart returned presently to the round man who was waiting at the door. "It's very interesting," he said. "I think I might enjoy painting as a hobby. There was one thing that puzzled me. I noticed that when they filled in the background all the students worked from left to right, sort of back-handed. Why is that?"

"It just happens that all the students in that particular class are right-handed," the round man answered. "Right-handed painters will nearly always make horizontal strokes from left to right. We learn to read and to write from left to right, you know. We observe most things from left to right. That's why captions on photographs always read from left to right. In the case of a left-handed painter, though, it's the exact opposite. His brush strokes would go from right to left."

"I see," said Hardin. "I'm interested in taking the course. You'll hear from me."

The round man warned Bart he should enroll early as the classes were filling up rapidly. He asked Hardin for his name. Bart gave a name. It wasn't Hardin.

The proprietor of the art school regarded Bart suspiciously as he left. Apparently he was accustomed to men wandering in for the sole purpose of getting a free look at a nude model.

Hardin walked down Eighth Street. A few doors west of the art school he came upon the Washington Square Bookshop. The shop was in an English basement, a step or two below street level. He pushed the door and entered a large, warm and pleasant room. Books, magazines and colorful greeting cards were arranged on shelves and racks. A coal fire was crackling in an old-fashioned grate. An intelligent-looking, dark-haired woman was drinking tea from a Wedgwood cup as she discharged her duties, at a desk beside the fireplace. She was charging out a rental copy for a customer as Bart went to the desk. She said, "You know the author of this book is a customer of ours. He got perfectly furious because we put it with the mysteries. He says it's a psychological novel. If it is, he must have a very bloody mind. There are *five* murders in it."

Bart waited his turn and did not become impatient with the delay, even when the dark-haired woman entered into a long discussion about the health and habits of her customer's cat. Several persons were browsing among the stacks of books, unhurriedly savoring sentences and paragraphs from different volumes. They had a look of tolerant contentment that was strikingly different from the expression of harried suspicion that seemed to be the mask of Broadway's people.

When the dark-haired woman finally turned to him, Bart asked her if she had copies of two plays in stock. She thought a minute and said, "I'm sure about one. But I'm afraid the trade edition of the other is out of print. I can give you a paperbacked reprint, though."

Bart told her that would serve his purpose. She went to the back of the shop and returned presently with the two books. Bart paid her, noting that his bankroll had now diminished almost to the point of outright disappearance. A couple more cab fares, he thought, and I'll be broke entirely. I'm not only broke, he reflected, I'm also unemployed.

There was no question of his continuing to work for a man who had believed he was a kidnapper and extortionist.

Bart thanked the woman, took the books she had inserted in a gray paper envelope and left the shop.

He walked to Sixth Avenue and flagged a cab. He had enough left to get uptown, anyway, with maybe a dollar or two to spare.

"Head for Times Square," he told the driver. "I'll tell you where to stop."

As the cab headed uptown, Bart took the two books from the envelope. One question had been answered at the art school. These books held the answer to another.

Hardin didn't really need to consult the books. He had

seen both of the plays performed and he was sure his memory was correct. But he wanted to check.

He had only to consult the cast of characters in the front of the first book to determine that he was right. The playwright had described each of his characters at great length.

He had to skim through the paperbacked volume before he came to the stage direction that he was seeking. He had been right there, too.

Hardin knew the identity of the murderer now and he knew the answer to Arlene's kidnapping.

But he needed twenty-five thousand dollars in cash to catch the killer.

thirteen

Hardin told the driver to let him off at the corner of Forty-ninth Street.

It was mid-afternoon when he paid the driver off and tipped him. He walked west on Jacobs Beach, toward Eighth Avenue. The street was thronged with shifty-looking citizens in wide-shouldered overcoats and wide-brimmed hats. Many of them were perusing folded race-track scratch sheets surreptitiously or were scanning the past-performance pages of the *Broadway Times*. Occasionally a man, whose air was so elaborately casual it would have attracted the suspicions of the most naïve policeman, sidled up to one of the loiterers and money changed hands.

Midway of the block, across from the Church of the Theatre, Bart came to a grimy store window that bore the legend, "Cigars, Cigarettes, Tobacco." Dummy cartons of cigarettes and cigar boxes had been placed in front of the baize curtain that hung on brass rings and shielded the interior of the establishment from public view. Bart opened the door of the shop. The lookout was a big, heavily jowled man named Eddie O'Grady. He sat behind the counter, posing as a tobacco salesman and Bart had often wondered what he would do if a customer actually entered with the intention of purchasing a pack of butts. On Broadway the aging lookout was called "The Old Top Sarge." He had won the Congressional Medal of Honor in the first World War and he wore the piece of metal on a star-spangled ribbon about his neck instead of a tie.

The Old Sarge beamed happily at Hardin. "Hello, Captain!" he exclaimed. "You gonna bang your head up against 'em again? I heard you dropped a bundle when that fuzzy wound up at the eighth pole the other day in Florida."

Bart said, "A week's salary plus a Christmas bonus. Is Selig in?"

The Old Sarge nodded and said, "He's in back." He pressed a button beneath the counter and a buzzer sounded, releasing the lock on a heavy door in the back of the store.

Back of the door was the most elaborate horse room in New York. It was the headquarters of Moe Selig. Selig ran all the gambling interests of the syndicate for Lenny Fassio, who was reputed to be the current boss. Selig also operated a loan-shark business in conjunction with his booking and gambling rackets. The two-buck bettors that thronged the street outside did not come in here. This room was reserved for the big gamblers, the professionals. Many of them were present now and they studied the illegal leased wires and the blackboards with the dedicated attention of Wall Street brokers on a big selling day.

The door was guarded by a large young hood whose

battered face indicated he had never learned to catch them on the glove. He knew Hardin, nodded to him.

Bart said, "I've got business with Selig."

The young hood said, "I'll knock."

Bart followed him to a closed door. The guard knocked at it, went inside. The hood came out, held the door slightly open, jerked his thumb toward the interior of the office. Bart entered.

Moe Selig was a balding man past middle age. He had slitted eyes and a large hooked nose. He was not tall but his shoulders were massive and his arms were disproportionately long, giving him a simian look. He sat behind his desk in his shirtsleeves, perusing a stack of account books. His shirt was white on white as usual. His collar was loosened and he had slipped the knot of his violently floral tie.

He nodded and said, "Hello, Hardin. You want to make a bet or you want to make a borrow? Or is this just a social call?"

Hardin said, "Business. I want to make a borrow."

Selig said, "Name it. Your credit's good with Selig. But even to friends the pay-off's six for five."

"How good is my credit?" Hardin asked.

Selig said, "When you make a borrow, you take the odds and you pay off. That makes your credit pretty good, I'd say. I don't like to have to send a boy for guys who make a borrow."

"I want twenty-five grand," Bart told him.

Selig's face remained impassive. He said, "I've heard

so many suckers crying when they blow a bet I got a tin ear, Hardin. Say it again."

"Twenty-five grand," Hardin repeated. "I want it in small bills if possible."

Selig said, "I didn't think I heard it right. Twenty-five gees ain't what they give the kiddies for mailing in their boxtops, Hardin. It costs thirty grand to make that kind of borrow."

Bart said, "I know that. You'll get your thirty grand inside twenty-four hours. That's five grand interest for using the dough a day instead of a week."

Selig leaned back in his swivel chair, put his hands behind his head and closed his heavy-lidded eyes. "Don't go away, Hardin," he said. "I'm thinking."

After he had thought a while, Selig spoke, with his eyes still closed. "I read newspapers," he said. "I read the afternoons I got here on my desk. Your boss paid off fifty gees to some snatchers. I never knew you to be in on a swindle before, but the only way I can figure it, you're in on a swindle now. The money's hot as the last bump in a stripper's grind. The serial numbers are printed in all the rags. I tore out the list myself, in case somebody tried to bet some of the double-saws in my book. Not that I'd holler copper—I'd just make a proposition, maybe."

Selig opened his eyes, looked at Bart. "I want to make a proposition, Hardin."

Bart said, "Make it."

Selig closed his eyes again. He said, "You found out this hot cabbage is up for sale, Hardin. It ain't like you, but that's the way it figures. So you want to make a buy. Twenty-five gees is too much for dough as hot as that is. I've made some buys before and you can take my word. Let 'em stew a little and by tomorrow they'll take ten, believe me. And you couldn't pass the warm lettuce. You ain't got the organization that Fassio and I have got. So maybe we can make a deal."

Selig opened his eyes again, regarded Hardin. "The deal is this," he said. "I give you fifteen gees in nice old dirty bills that nobody can trace. You pay the chumps ten, or less, maybe, and you keep the change. Whatever you save is your commission. The hot cabbage comes to us and we're the ones who have to pass it."

Bart said, "No deal. I want to make a borrow. A twenty-five grand borrow. I'll pay it back with five grand interest by tomorrow."

Selig shook his head. "It ain't that I don't trust you, Hardin. But there's one big hitch. I wouldn't take the thirty grand in bills that had the serial numbers that are printed in the paper."

"They won't be those bills," Hardin replied. "Twenty-five thousand dollars' worth will be in the bills you give to me. The other five will be a check that you won't refuse."

Selig closed his eyes again and he thought a long time before he answered.

Finally he said, "I like to keep on the good side of newsboys, Hardin. I know you ain't on the take, you've had plenty of chances for that. But sometimes I put money in a night club or a play and if the newsboys owe me favors

it might help a little with publicity. You might not believe it, but I don't back only girlie shows. The producers
don't know the money comes from me, but sometimes
I back a lot of long-hair stuff. On account of my wife. It
makes her proud of me. She's a great admirer of those
highbrow plays. My wife's a real intelligent woman. She
reads magazines."

Hardin waited.

Selig opened his eyes and stared hard at Bart. He said,
"You're getting into something, Hardin. You couldn't
ever pass it. But it ain't my business. I may get hell from
Fassio, but maybe I'll play along. This is the proposition.
Number one, you don't pay me back in hot bills. Number
two, the interest on this borrow is five thousand dollars
a day, not six for five a week the way it usually is. Number
three, you pay me the dough or the interest on it at this
time tomorrow afternoon. I told you once I'd never send
a boy for you. You ain't the type I send a boy for, not if
the borrow's a few C-notes or maybe a grand. But for
twenty-five grand, I'll send a boy, Hardin. I'll send a real
big boy. Maybe two. Fassio and I have got a lot of real big
boys. And the things they do ain't nice."

Bart said, "It's a deal."

Selig shook his head. "I shouldn't do it. It's gonna make
Lenny Fassio mighty mad at me. I've lasted in this racket
more than thirty years because I haven't made guys like
Fassio mad. But the main reason I shouldn't do it is I like
you, Hardin. I wouldn't like to send a boy for you. You
don't know what it's like, maybe, when one of the boys
drops around for a little chat."

Hardin said, "I've got a good imagination. I've heard what happened to a few guys when the boys dropped in for a little chat. I want to make the borrow."

Selig shrugged his massive shoulders. "All right," he said. "You're supposed to be a smart. You're an editor. You got an education. I only went through reform school myself, but I'd have better sense if I was you. How you want the loot?"

"Twenties will do," Hardin answered.

Selig picked up one of the four phones on his desk and said, "Send in Blake."

Blake was a thin, pasty-faced man. He wore a green eye-shade and paper sleeveguards.

Selig said to him, "Get me twenty-five grand in double-saws. And put it in a paper shopping bag."

Blake merely nodded, left the office.

Selig chuckled. "There ain't nothing looks as innocent as a paper shopping bag," he said, "unless it's a chump who thinks he's got inside information on a fixed horse-race. It's the way the boys carry dough when they take the pay-off to the books and numbers stations all over town. Some of the boys get real fancy. They put a bunch of car-rots or a head of cabbage on top of the money in the bag."

"Never mind the vegetables," Bart replied. "All I want is twenty-five thousand dollars."

Ten minutes elapsed before Blake reappeared. Selig said, "Don't get impatient, Hardin. Blake is a very care-ful guy. He was a bank teller a long time ago but he gave the boss a fast count once and he wound up doing an

184

embezzlement rap. With me, he always counts nice and slow."

When Blake brought the money in, he took it from the bag and counted it over nice and slow in front of Hardin.

Hardin stuffed the money in the bag.

He walked to the door, called over his shoulder to Selig, "I'll see you tomorrow about this time. Or maybe even earlier."

Selig said, "I hope you do, chum. For your own sake, I hope to hell you do."

fourteen

Bart left the bookie shop and stood for a moment on Jacobs Beach. He looked around him, trying to spot the gray Chevvy that Romano had pointed out in front of the Sutton Hospital. He did not see it.

He did not see a stocky man and a lean man who were mingling with the horse players and bookie's runners on the street either. They differed little from the other loiterers except that the shoulders of their overcoats were not quite so heavily padded and the brims of their hats were not quite so wide.

Not seeing the two men was Hardin's first mistake.

Bart wanted to call Romano and he wondered if the lieutenant had returned to Manhattan West. He glanced at his watch, saw it was a little after four. Hardin never took a drink before four o'clock in the afternoon. It was one of the few small disciplines he observed in his generally disorganized existence. He wanted a drink now. The Sligo Slasher's Bar was just across Eighth Avenue. He decided he could have his drink and make the call from there.

Not calling Romano immediately was Hardin's second mistake.

The fat man sidled up to the lean man. He said softly, "He's got two bags now. The one he got in the bookstore and a big shopping bag."

The lean man said just as softly, "I wonder what he's got inside it?"

The fat man shrugged his meaty shoulders, nudged his companion forward as Hardin turned toward Eighth Avenue. "When Selig's boys make the rounds of bookie joints and numbers banks they carry the payoff in paper sacks," he said.

"Maybe we better call up if we get a chance," the lean man suggested.

The fat man said, "Maybe. Drift across the street. We don't want to lose him now."

Hardin went into the Sligo Slasher's Bar and headed for the one phone booth. Tony Maclaren called loudly, "Hey, ya Protestant bum! The bar's this way." The Sligo Slasher poured a hefty shot of Irish into an old-fashioned glass, slammed it on the bar. "First one's on the house," he said. "Drink up."

Hardin grinned at the Slasher, walked to the bar and picked up the glass. He drank a little of the whiskey.

Taking the drink was Hardin's third mistake.

The fat man and the lean man had entered the bar together. The lean man nodded toward the phone booth. The fat man walked to the phone booth, entered it, closed the folding door. The lean man stood at the bar between Hardin and the street door. He ordered a short beer.

Hardin took another sip from the whiskey, found change and turned toward the phone booth. It was occupied now. He walked back to the bar and picked up the drink. He had finished the drink when he heard the door of the phone booth slam open. He walked toward the phone.

The fat man who had just come out of the booth blocked Hardin's path.

Bart tried to steer around him.

The fat man moved slightly, cutting off the booth. He nodded toward the lean man at the bar, who walked slowly toward Hardin and the fat man.

The fat man took a leather-cased badge from a pocket, showed it to Hardin, shielding it with his hand. He said, "Police. We're working out of the district attorney's office. I've got orders to take you in."

Hardin had folded over the top portion of the hefty bag, containing the money. He was holding it under his arm. Involuntarily his arm squeezed down hard on the well-filled shopping bag.

He said, "Why?"

The lean man who had come up behind him spoke. He said, "We just take 'em in. We don't answer questions, mister. Come on."

Bart said, "I want to make a phone call."

"Maybe the D.A. will let you make one. He's a real obliging character," the fat man said, putting his hand lightly against Hardin's crooked elbow. "Come on."

Hardin said, "I want to call a cop."

The fat man gave a short laugh. "You got two cops, buddy. That's enough."

"Where are we going?" Bart asked desperately. "I've already seen the D.A. today."

"He likes you," the lean man answered. "He wants to see you again." He urged Bart toward the door.

The fat man picked up the gray envelope containing the books that Bart had left on the bar. He handed it to Hardin and said affably, "Don't forget your package."

Bart shook the detective's hand from his arm and said, "I didn't pay for my drink."

He pushed to the bar, put a dollar on the mahogany. Maclaren was staring at Hardin and the two detectives, his mouth hanging open. Customers at the bar were also watching with intent interest, their glasses halfway to their mouths.

Hardin spoke rapidly. He said, "You know Romano. Call him at Manhattan West. Tell him I can't keep our appointment. Tell him the D.A. has taken me into custody."

The fat man jerked Hardin and this time he wasn't gentle. He said, "You're a real cute character. I don't think the lieutenant is going to fight City Hall even if he is your friend." He looked menacingly at Maclaren. "I noticed quite a few violations when I came in here," he said. "For one thing, the joint's a firetrap. You need an automatic sprinkler system that'll cost a grand or two. I wouldn't make that call if I wanted to keep my license."

He shoved Bart toward the door.

The gray Chevvy coupe was parked inconspicuously around the corner. The three men climbed in. Bart was in the middle.

The lean man drove. The fat man was on Bart's right. He was so wide he sat sideways, his broad buttocks wedged against the door of the coupe.

As the car headed downtown the detectives talked about a fight they'd seen at the St. Nick Arena the week before. They didn't address Hardin once.

They parked the car in front of a building on Leonard Street in downtown New York, on the edge of the canyon-like financial district. They took Bart into a small office where the redhead, Saltus, was waiting.

"Which is the package he picked up at the place on Forty-ninth?" Saltus asked eagerly.

"The big one under his arm," the fat detective answered. "The little bag's the one he got in the bookstore. I touched it. It feels like books."

"Believe it or not, some bookstores still sell books," Bart said.

"What's in the big package?" Saltus asked.

The lean man said, "We didn't look, sir. That's your responsibility."

Saltus said to Hardin, "Put it on the desk."

Hardin said, "I don't think you've got a right to look at either one of the packages. They're personal property."

Saltus grinned unpleasantly, crinkling the freckles on his face into rusty splotches. "That's where we disagree," he said. "I think we have the right and we're going to look.

190

But I'll be glad to write it in the record that you're an upstanding citizen who's jealous of his constitutional rights, if that will help. Put the package on the desk, Hardin."

Hardin said, "I demand to make a phone call."

That seemed to please Saltus, too. He grinned again. "I'm afraid I can't grant you that permission. It's out of my hands now, and I don't have the authority. Maybe the district attorney, Mr. Broderick, will let you make the call. He wants to talk to you, but he wants to know what's in the package first. I doubt Marty Land could help you much, anyway. Dragging another bum out of a flophouse to testify in your behalf would be a bit too much now. Put that package on the desk."

Hardin didn't protest further. There wasn't any use. He laid the shopping bag on the desk in front of Saltus. Saltus looked inside and smiled happily. He turned the shopping bag upside down and the banded package of twenty-dollar bills tumbled out onto the desk. A few bounced to the floor. The lean detective picked them up.

Saltus counted the money hurriedly. "Why, it seems there's just about twenty-five thousand dollars here. All in twenties, too! Where'd you get all this money, Hardin?"

Bart said, "I don't think I'm required to answer that unless I'm asked by the boys from Internal Revenue."

Saltus turned to his two detectives and said with heavy-handed humor, "Isn't it just wonderful the way the average citizen knows his rights nowadays? It's an enlightened age we live in." He turned to Hardin and said, "We might have the right ourselves, though, if they were ransom bills paid out in a kidnapping."

"Why don't you check them? The serial numbers of the ransom bills are in all the afternoon papers. It only costs a nickel to buy a paper. New York County would doubtless reimburse you for the expenditure."

Saltus addressed his aides again. "This man is very intelligent," he said mockingly. "He anticipates my every move. That's just what I'm going to do."

He put the packages of money back into the bag, handed the bag to the fat man. "Take those out and check them against the list," he directed.

The fat detective left the room, carrying the money.

Bart said, "I'd like a receipt."

"All in good time," Saltus answered. "We always give a man a receipt for his property when we hold him on any charge. That's just routine."

"Is it against the law to carry twenty-five thousand dollars in a paper bag?" Hardin asked.

"No," said Saltus. "It isn't. It's just kind of careless."

Saltus picked up the phone and said, "Give me the district attorney." He waited a moment, then he said, "We've got Hardin, sir. He was carrying a paper bag. He got the paper bag at that place on Forty-ninth. There's twenty-five thousand dollars in twenty-dollar bills in the paper bag."

Bart could hear a muffled clacking in the receiver as Broderick answered. Saltus said, "Of course, sir. Right away."

The assistant district attorney rose and said to Bart, "You're a lucky boy. The district attorney is going to give you his personal attention. This way, please."

He led Bart down a corridor. The lean detective followed, directly behind Hardin. Saltus stuck his head into an office and said to a girl who was pounding a typewriter, "Tell Griffin to bring his report to the D.A.'s office."

They went into a large anteroom where secretaries and clerks were working. A uniformed policeman stood guard at a heavy inner door. Saltus led the way through the door.

The district attorney's private office was also large. It was cluttered with furniture and glass-front bookcases holding weighty tomes. The walls were decorated by oil portraits and photographs of gentlemen who wore a conscientiously judicial look.

Broderick was a small, wiry man with crinkly hair, heavy eyebrows and a red Irish face. He said at once, "You're Mr. Hardin? Please take a chair."

Hardin sat down.

Broderick's keen eyes wandered over him, sizing him up, as a fighter might size up his opponent when he lolls in his corner before the bell.

Broderick said, "Do you want to tell us about it, Mr. Hardin? Or do we ask you questions? Either way you like."

Bart said, "Tell you what?"

Broderick nodded, accepting it. "I see we ask questions," he said. "For one thing, I suggest you tell us how it happens you visited a resort of known hoodlums a lit-

193

tle while ago and emerged with a paper bag containing twenty-five thousand dollars."

"Do you know the place I visited is a resort of hoodlums?" Bart asked. "If you do, why don't you close it down? It's been doing business at the same old stand for fifteen years at least."

Broderick nodded and smiled affably at Hardin. "We are reasonably sure it is a resort of hoodlums, Mr. Hardin. I won't deny you have a point. The cigar store is a front for the headquarters of Moe Selig. It is the focal point of all the illegal gambling enterprises in New York County. It has been raided several times, as you doubtless know, especially during the early days of reform administrations that have promised to clean the town up overnight. You can't clean this town up overnight. It's too big. The raids have produced proof of bookmaking —leased wires, innumerable telephones, betting slips, scratch sheets, blackboards with race results. We have rounded up patrol wagons full of men who were charged with the misdemeanor of illegal gambling. We have even caught Selig a time or two and on each occasion he has maintained he was there solely to place an illegal bet on a horse, a minor crime punishable by a fine or a few days in jail. All the weight of evidence we can bring to court always shows that a minor mobster, paid by the Syndicate to front and take the rap, has been proprietor of the establishment. We don't want minor mobsters any more than we want the little men who make book in candy stores. We want men like Selig and Fassio. So far we haven't got them with anything that can stick. We could go right on raiding and make such a nuisance they would move from their present address and set up business a block or two east or west or north or south. We'd rather have them where they are. We can watch them better that way. My approach to law enforcement is more realistic than idealistic, I'm afraid. I've answered your question. Would you care to answer mine?"

Bart said, "If you can't make it stick against Selig, I doubt there's anything will stick against me. I went into a known resort of gamblers, a bookie joint. I came out with a bag full of money. The obvious inference is I won it."

"You wish to state you won the money?" Broderick asked quickly.

"I didn't state that. I merely said it was an obvious inference," Bart replied.

"There is another inference," Broderick said. "I think it is a better one, if you will permit me an opinion. You have been closely identified with a chain of events that have resulted in two murders and a kidnapping. The inference I might make is that you were an accomplice of hoodlums in these events and that the money you carried from a resort of known hoodlums was your share of the ransom money paid by Maddox Slade, your employer, in the kidnapping of his wife."

The fat detective named Griffin came through the door. Hardin looked up at him, said, "Here's the man who has the answer to that, I think."

"Did you check?" asked Saltus eagerly.

"It'll take a while," the detective answered. "But I've

got four men on it and we've checked a lot of the bills. They don't match the serials of the ransom money. My guess is that none of them will."

Broderick said to Bart, "This doesn't clear you, Mr. Hardin. It merely proves that you are clever. I can visualize two possibilities. One is that you were an accomplice of the hoodlums, a kind of finger-man and go-between and that you refused to take your share in bills whose serial numbers were listed. The second is that you were acting alone, had the entire fifty thousand in bills whose serial numbers were listed. You were afraid to try to pass them. So you sold them to the Syndicate for half their face value. Any statement, Mr. Hardin?"

"Yes," said Bart. "I'd like to make a phone call."

Broderick said, "I shan't prevent you, Mr. Hardin. But I will make a suggestion in all good faith. As a lawyer, I suggest to you that you wait until I make a charge before calling your attorney. That way, he can proceed more intelligently in seeing you are not deprived of your legal rights."

"You're going to book me?" Bart asked. "What charge?"

"There are several that occur to me. Suspicion of murder is one. Accessory in kidnapping and extortion is another. Or I could merely hold you as a material witness until I decide."

"I didn't want to call a lawyer," Bart said. "I wanted to call a cop. Lieutenant Romano at Manhattan West."

Broderick said, "In that case there is no need for you to make a call. Lieutenant Romano called me shortly after you were picked up. Someone had informed him

196

you were in custody. He is probably in the outside office now. I told him he could come down and I would call on him if he were needed."

"Get him in here," Bart urged. "If you'll play ball, I think I can deliver the murderer and the people behind the kidnapping to you tonight."

Broderick's eyes appraised Bart. He said, "That's a bold promise, Mr. Hardin. I have no objection to Romano sitting in on this. There is no jealousy between his office and mine. We work together. My assistants always work with Homicide men on a case to make sure the evidence they gather is sufficient in a legal sense to bring a case to court. But if you are willing to talk to Lieutenant Romano, why aren't you willing to talk to us? We're on the same team, you know."

"Because I think Romano will do it my way and I don't think you would," Bart answered. "And if it isn't done my way, it won't get done at all."

Broderick clicked an intercom on his desk, spoke into it, asked if Romano was waiting in the outer office. When he learned the lieutenant was there, he told the girl to send him in.

Romano shuffled in, walking as if his feet hurt. He nodded to the men in the room. He spied a water carafe on the district attorney's desk, picked it up and said, "You don't mind if I take a slug of this do you?" He poured water into a glass, produced a small metal box from his pocket and proferred it to the D.A. "Have a soda tablet?" he asked. "I ate a pastrami sandwich a little while ago. I shouldn't have. Pastrami always makes me burp."

197

Romano swallowed his pill, sat down in a chair.

Broderick looked at Bart. "I believe you wanted to make a statement, Mr. Hardin," he said.

Hardin said, "No. I wanted to make a proposition. Maybe it's presumption to make a proposition to the District Attorney of New York County. If it is, I'm sorry. I'm going to make one. The proposition's this. Give me back my paper bag of money. Let me out of here in the custody of Lieutenant Romano. He can stay with me every minute. It's a little after five now. By tonight I think I can hand you a murderer and the explanation of everything that's happened."

"He's stalling," said Saltus.

"It's quite impossible," said Broderick. "It's too irregular. It's asking the lieutenant to assume too much responsibility. That's unfair. Anything you have to say, any explanations you have to make, can be said and made right here and now. I'm tired of fooling with you, Hardin. I've already given you a lot of leeway."

"That's all I have to say, then," Bart answered. "What I might say or explain right now wouldn't mean a thing. It's what Romano and I would do in the next few hours that would count."

"Excuse me," Romano said. "This joker could be leveling. I know him pretty well. I knew his dad and I've known Hardin since he was a punk. He's got a lot of faults. When he clams up, he's clammed and you might as well quit. He's got a head made out of cement. He plays marbles his way or he don't play at all. He means it now. Maybe you can make something stick if it's Hardin you

198

want something to stick against. I don't know. But I ought to tell you something. After you told me Hardin came out of Selig's joint with a big paper bundle, I called up Selig. Selig and I aren't friends, but we talk together now and then. Selig swears he lent Hardin a hunk of money, just because Hardin is an old pal. What he did was lend it at six for five, of course, but I wouldn't ask him to admit that. If you want to make something out of the money, you got Selig's testimony to contend with. I never heard of a law against making a friendly loan."

Broderick said, "Are you suggesting I play along and let you take the responsibility for this man?"

Romano shrugged. "It's up to you," he said. "Something might pop. If it doesn't I can always bring him back. A few hours can't make much difference, anyway."

"You would be assuming a grave responsibility, Lieutenant," the district attorney warned Romano.

"I been leading with my chin in this job so long it don't even hurt much any more," Romano answered.

Broderick drummed fingers on his desk. Finally he said. "All right. If that's the way you want it, I'll play along. I have reason to respect your judgment, Lieutenant. But for your sake I hope nothing goes wrong. If it does, you know the possible consequences, I suppose."

Romano nodded heavily. "I know," he said. "I guess I could start up a bee farm, maybe. That's what Sherlock Holmes did when he retired. Only I don't like honey very much. And I got poisoned from a bee sting once when I was a kid."

Broderick said to the fat detective, "Get Hardin's money."

"It won't be all checked yet," the detective replied.

"It doesn't matter. If they haven't found ransom bills by now, they're not likely to find any," Broderick said.

Saltus had carried the gray envelope containing the two books into the office. He was still holding it. Bart said, "I'd like my books back, too. They're as important as the money."

Broderick looked at Hardin curiously. "Give the man his books," he said to Saltus.

Hardin took the books. When the detective brought in the shopping bag filled with currency, Bart said, "You take it, Lieutenant. If anything happens to me, give it back to Selig. I owe it to him."

The Buick was parked in front of the building, but Grierson wasn't driving. As Romano started up the motor, he asked, "Where to?"

"We've got to talk a little bit first," Bart replied. "Your office is as good a place as any."

"I hope you're sure what you're doing," Romano said. "I've got a kind of glimmering, but that's all."

"I'm sure of one thing," Bart declared. "If this doesn't work out, I'll be glad to go to jail. About this time tomorrow, Selig will be sending a couple of boys for me. A couple of real big boys."

fifteen

They were back in the little room with the green-shaded light now, Romano's cubbyhole at Manhattan West.

The lieutenant hung his bulky, rumpled overcoat carelessly on the clothes tree. Another coat was there on a hanger. It was blue and well tailored and it looked new. Romano pointed to it and said, "How you like my Christmas present? It's real fancy. One hundred percent cashmere. My wife and daughter gave it to me for a Christmas present. They got tired of waiting for me to come home for Christmas. I been sleeping on that old leather couch ever since Drake got bumped. So my daughter brought the present down to me this afternoon."

Hardin said, "It's too elegant for a cop. They'll think you're in on a shakedown if you wear that around."

Romano sat down in a swivel chair, loosened his shoestrings and sighed heavily. "You seem pretty cocky about this business," he said. "Pretty sure of what you're doing. That's why I stuck my chin out for you. There's only one thing I'm pretty sure about."

"What?" asked Hardin.

"I'm pretty sure that Mrs. Maddox Slade wasn't kidnapped," Romano replied.

Bart nodded. "That's the key to it," he agreed. "Only it's a key that fits too damned many doors Almost from the start I was pretty sure myself. I was pretty sure that it was Slade behind it all."

Romano said, "Yeah. I figured that was the way your mind was working."

"It seemed to fit," Bart continued. "It seemed to fit almost all the way. Slade never asked me up to his house for social visits, but he asked me up for Christmas Eve. So I thought he had an angle. At first I thought his angle was using me to bully a little man who'd cheated his wife out of five thousand bucks. Then I began to believe it was because he wanted me to be there when the first note arrived, the note that said Arlene had been kidnapped while she was sitting right there with us. I thought Slade sent that note, or had it sent, and timed it to arrive when I was present so it would plant the idea in my head that Arlene was in danger of being snatched."

Bart shook his head and said, "I had a real nice theory and for a while nearly all the facts fitted it perfectly. Slade was jealous of his wife. Drake was blackmailing Arlene. I thought he hadn't been satisfied with the five thousand she gave him for the painting of the flying ducks and had gone to Slade and told him the whole story of her affair with this young actor, Barnaby. Slade knew Drake was a crook, a blackmailer. So he planned to use him. As he said himself, men like Drake come cheap. He dreamed up a fake kidnapping. He had Drake write the three kidnap notes. Drake could have mailed the first one, the one that came to Gracie Square, himself. He could have left the second one behind the gun counter of the shooting gallery a minute before he was murdered. He could have given the third, the one delivered in the brief case, to Slade to use when he saw fit.

"I thought Slade planned the kidnapping hoax to cover up the murder of his wife. I had everything explained, almost, up to a certain point. He had me go after her to 'protect' her when she stormed out of the apartment on Christmas Eve. He was pretty sure I'd bring her to my apartment, I suppose. That would be convenient for the appointment in the shooting gallery he knew she had at midnight. He knew it because he'd had Drake call her and make the appointment. At least that was my theory. The time element bothered me, though. Drake was killed just before midnight. Slade was in the shooting gallery, but Arlene wasn't with him then and she wasn't in my apartment. There were two ways of explaining that. He had called my apartment earlier, when Arlene was there and I was out, and arranged to meet her and kill her and come back to the shooting gallery and shoot Drake after he put the letter behind the counter. Or he could have met Arlene, in the shooting gallery a few minutes before twelve, had her wait in a parked car while he went back and took care of Drake and killed her at his leisure and dumped the body on some country road.

"All the calls I received from the kidnapper could have been Slade himself, using a disguised voice. He had to kill Drake, of course, because he knew Drake was a black-mailer and Drake would have known he'd murdered his wife. I didn't drop the theory when the brief case was delivered by Old Fats dressed up like Santa Claus. Slade certainly couldn't risk too many accomplices, but he might have risked a bum he met on the street who had nothing to do but bring a brief case up to me. I thought he'd bribed Old Fats to say a little old lady in widow's weeds had given him the package. There was other corroborative evidence. Slade panicked when he heard he had been seen in the shooting gallery and that the police wanted to talk to him. He ran away and hid. He didn't want to list the serial numbers of the bills. I figured that was because he'd arranged to recover the bills and didn't want them traced to him. Carberry Payne remembered something about the brief case, something that cost him his life. He remembered he'd seen Drake carrying it. That fit, too. Drake could have bought the case for Slade, since he was already in on the plan and was going to be eliminated anyway. And Slade got unreasonably furious when he learned I'd planted old James Lennox in the theatre to watch the brief case. Also, I thought he was afraid I would go to the police before his plans were worked out and that this was the reason he put a tail on me and tried to make me the goat in the kidnapping."

"So Mrs. Slade comes back," Romano said. "She's alive, so he couldn't have murdered her. And you've wasted a lot of time on some real smart thinking."

"That clinched it, of course," Bart admitted. "But my theory was dead before that happened, even. I had no way of explaining how Slade got the money back. I couldn't imagine him using another accomplice. Then when I found Payne had the brief case and could have taken the money out, I thought it barely possible he was working with Slade, only I just couldn't believe he was the kind of man who would do that. Payne's murder, though, left some doubt. Slade might have killed him to keep him quiet. But there were objections. The man Old Fats described as being in the bar and looking through the window and entering the Weird Things shop certainly could have been Slade. The thing that really knocked the theory all to hell, though, was my interview with the little usher, Violet Brent."

"Why?"

"She told me that a little woman with a limp, dressed in mourning clothes, bought the ticket for my seat. The same kind of little woman that Old Fats had described. Either both Old Fats and Violet were lying or Slade had another accomplice. He already had used Drake and Old Fats in the scheme. I just couldn't imagine him hiring some woman, too. It wasn't in character. Slade is a very careful man."

"So I really have led with my chin, if that's all you got," Romano commented. "It couldn't have been Slade. That's all you know, really. Even a dumb cop could figure that. I figured it. I figured that and I figured the kidnap was a fake. I knew it was a fake because of the way Mrs. Slade was acting. It wasn't a very good act for an actress. She claimed she lost her memory because somebody conked her on the head when she left your apartment, or doped her, maybe. There wasn't any mark on her head, just the black eye, and a black eye doesn't make you lose your memory for three days. It wasn't likely anybody would have doped her right there in the hall of an apartment house, especially one with an outside door that's never locked. Doping takes a little time. I've seen a lot of amnesia victims. That act wasn't any good, either. If she'd stuck to her first story, that she didn't even know her own name, she might have got by with it. Or if she'd pretended she knew who she was but just couldn't remember the events of the last few days, she might have got by with that. But she couldn't get by with both. If she'd blacked out completely, she wouldn't recover her memory in an hour or two and still just have a blank spot about the last few days. She should have read up on amnesia in some case histories before she put her act on."

Romano slipped his foot out of a shoe and began to massage it tenderly. "I tried to give you a break, but I'll have to take you back," he said. "You don't know anything after all. You were only bluffing the D.A. I can't say I blame you too much, though. It was worth a try, I guess."

Bart said, "I know who murdered Drake and Payne and who is behind the kidnapping scheme."

"You *know?*" asked Romano. "You're a whole lot smarter than I am, then. I've maybe got suspicions but I can't prove a thing."

"I'm not smarter," Bart said. "It just happens I attend the theatre in the line of duty. You don't. I attended three plays in particular, and I remembered something from each of them that's significant. I checked part of what I remembered in these two books." Bart tapped his hand on the gray envelope containing the two books he had bought at the Washington Square shop.

Romano looked puzzled. He said, "So you've got another theory. I hope it's better than the first one. Can you prove anything?"

"I think I can," Bart answered. "I can if you'll help me."

"What do you want me to do?"

"I want you to come with me to a certain place and pretend you're one of Moe Selig's muscle men."

"My muscles are going kind of flabby these days," the lieutenant said. "But the older I get, the uglier I get. Maybe I'm almost as ugly as one of Selig's goons."

"Tell me something," said Bart. "Did one of your questioned-documents men see those kidnap notes?"

"Yeah. Only he couldn't tell us much except the guy who printed them was left-handed. Even a chump like me could guess that by just looking at them."

Bart nodded. "A chump like me saw that, too. Slade was right-handed. Carberry Payne wrote down an address for me. He was right-handed. That's why I figured Drake must have written all the notes. I didn't know whether he was left-handed or right-handed, so I assumed he was the left-handed man in the deal. Today I found out Drake was right-handed, too."

"How?"

"Drake smeared the paint on heavy in that picture of the ducks that Arlene bought from him. It's easy to see the direction of the brush strokes. I even commented upon that when Slade asked me to tell him what I thought about the painting. The brush strokes go from left to right. Drake was careless, too. He must have painted the picture in a hurry. He didn't even hit the end of the can-

207

vas with some of the strokes. There's white spaces all along the right edge of the painting. Today I went down to the Village and watched a group of art students working. They all made their horizontal strokes from left to right. The proprietor of the school said that was because they were right-handed. He said right-handed people nearly always painted that way. He said a left-handed painter would make his strokes just the opposite. So Drake was right-handed and didn't write the notes the way I'd believed he had."

"What's that got to do with these plays you saw?" Romano asked.

"I found the left-handed man in one of the plays," Bart answered. "The play I saw last night at Opportunity, Incorporated. It was a production of Tennessee Williams *Camino Réal*. When a character named Kilroy makes his first entrance, he turns and writes with chalk on a set that's supposed to be a stone wall. Howard Barnaby played Kilroy last night. He wrote on the wall with his left hand. He was holding up the set with his right hand, in fact, so it was especially noticeable."

Romano made an indecisive sound in his throat, waited.

"On Christmas morning, when he delivered the package to me, Old Fats swore it had been given to him by a little woman in mourning clothes who walked with a limp," Bart went on. "Last night Carberry Payne told me that the only parts Violet Brent had ever played at Opportunity, Incorporated were those of Martha Brewster, one of the crazy sisters who lure old men to their house and murder them in Kesselring's *Arsenic and Old Lace*, and Laura, in Williams' *Glass Menagerie.* He also said his kids had to supply their own costumes."

Bart took the two books out of the gray envelope, opened the one bound in paper. He thumbed through the pages until he found the place he wanted. "Listen to this," he said. "It's a stage direction from Act 2 of *Arsenic and Old Lace.*"

Bart read from the book, " 'We see Abby and Martha on the balcony. They are dressed for Mr. Hoskins' funeral. Mr. Hoskins is being paid the respect of deep and elaborate mourning.' "

Bart opened the hard-cover to the Cast of Charcters "Williams describes his characters in *The Glass Menagerie* at great length," he said. "Here is the playwright's own description of Laura Wingfield, the part that Violet Brent played in the Opportunity, Incorporated production: 'A childhood illness has left her crippled, one leg slightly shorter than the other.' "

There was silence as Romano thought about it and massaged his foot. "Go on," the lieutenant said at length.

"If Violet Brent had any reason to assume a disguise, she would naturally use the costume she had at hand and add to it any mannerisms she had already practiced in parts she'd played," he said. "She probably powdered her face heavily and put in wrinkles with a makeup pencil and wore spectacles and even at that hid her face behind a thick black veil when she went uptown on Christmas morning to make sure the brief case was delivered. She assumed the limp she had used in the role of Laura in another play. She wrapped the brief case in some Christmas paper she had purchased from Payne's shop, paper that ironically enough had been designed by Drake. She wasn't quite up to facing me in person. She planned to get someone to take it up for her. She ran into a man dressed like Santa Claus right outside my flat and it seemed a perfect setup. She gave him a big tip to deliver the package to me. Of course, no limping little lady in black bought the ticket that was sent to me. When I asked Violet if she remembered the person she had sold the ticket to, she figured I had probably asked Old Fats who gave him the package to deliver, so she embroidered the story to make it convincing. Actually, she pulled the ticket from the rack and gave it to Barnaby."

"You realize you're saying this kid is an accomplice in kidnapping and murder," Romano remarked.

"That's what I couldn't believe," Bart answered. "She's one of the most genuinely sweet youngsters I've met in a long time. I don't think she knew what she was doing. I even think I know what Barnaby told her. I think I can guess partly because I'm in it and Slade's in it and Arlene's in it. I think Barnaby pretended it was all a big publicity hoax that might get him a fat part on Broadway if she would help him. She was crazy in love with him, and when a stage-struck kid like that is in love with a big, handsome actor like Barnaby, she's not likely to think too clearly. Besides, Violet's a lot more naïve than she pretends to be. I think Barnaby persuaded her that Arlene was staging this fake kidnapping of herself, that her husband, who backs shows and runs a theatrical paper, was going to pay a ransom and that Barnaby was going to save Arlene, recover the ransom and be a hero. He told her that would put him in solid with Slade and assure his theatrical future. I think she fell for something about like that."

"It would be pretty hard to explain the murders to her, or why Slade didn't get the ransom money back," Romano commented.

"Barnaby didn't plan any murders. He had to commit them because his plan went haywire. Maybe Barnaby thought his sex appeal was sufficient to make Violet run away with him after he had the money. Or maybe he just planned to run away himself and let her do her worst. And there's one more possibility. It isn't pleasant."

"What?"

"He's planning to kill Violet Brent before he's through."

Romano said, "You've got a lot of fancy theories. You haven't got a single fact the D.A. is going to buy."

"Let me tell it from the first," Bart urged. "I think I've got a way of making the D.A. buy it. Barnaby had been intimate with Arlene before her marriage. When she married Slade, he thought he was set. He thought Arlene would be able to support him in a style to which he wasn't accustomed. But she couldn't give him money because Slade gave her only a niggardly cash allowance. Barnaby didn't believe that. He thought Arlene was holding out on him. He had letters from her. He may have even made tape recordings when she was there. But he didn't want to blackmail her himself. His roommate, Drake, was a little guy and he bullied him. Drake was penniless. Barnaby pretended to have a quarrel with

Drake and moved out. Then he gave Drake the material to blackmail Arlene. When the picture deal went through, Barnaby was finally convinced Arlene was telling the truth, that she had no access to real money. He persuaded Arlene that if they could shake Slade down for a large amount of cash, they could run away together. So they cooked up this fake kidnapping scheme between them. Arlene would meet Barnaby in the shooting gallery at midnight and go to a place he'd arranged in New Haven until the ransom was paid. Then they'd leave the country together. They thought they were safe enough. If Slade found out his wife had extorted fifty thousand dollars from him and run away with another man, he wasn't likely to make the fact public. He had too much pride for that, they figured.

"Barnaby needed an accomplice, so he dragged in Drake again. He knew Drake was scared to death of him and could be bullied into anything. He needed him to deliver the notes and pick up the ransom. But Drake balked. He was afraid to go to Slade or the police, but he wanted no part of a capital crime like kidnapping, even if it was a fake. I suspect he was sore at Barnaby, too, because he'd been cheated of his share of the money Arlene paid for the painting. He thought he had a way of spiking Barnaby's guns. He was supposed to mail the first kidnap note that Barnaby had written so it would reach Slade Christmas morning. He would have delivered the brief case to me late that afternoon or Christmas night under the original plan. But he mailed the special delivery letter so it would reach Slade on Christmas Eve, before his wife had disappeared. He thought that would tip Slade off. I was with Slade when the note arrived. He treated it as a bad joke.

"Arlene was in a spot. She was frantic to get out of there and try to get in touch with Barnaby after the note arrived. So she made a scene and stormed out. She probably went to a phone and couldn't reach Barnaby because he was on stage. She couldn't go down to the theatre and be seen with him. She was supposed to meet him at midnight. That's what the memo that fell out of her purse meant— a date with Barnaby, not a date with Drake, as she said. It was the note that sent Slade to the shooting gallery. Barnaby had chosen the shooting gallery because it was a good place to leave the note to me. If I didn't go down when he called, he could be pretty sure that whoever picked it up would deliver it to me upstairs.

"When Arlene couldn't get Barnaby on the phone, she took a cab and waited for me in Gracie Square. She thought she would wait in my apartment until she could reach Barnaby. Maybe she faked passing out, although Lord knows she had enough liquor to pass her out. Maybe she figured that would get me out of the flat so she could use the phone again. Anyway, I left and she called Barnaby and caught him this time and told him what had happened. He told her to get out of there, probably to take a late train to New Haven and he'd meet her there as soon as he could.

"Barnaby had to make new plans and he had to work fast. He got hold of Drake, because he knew Drake had double-crossed him and had to be killed. He forced Drake

213

to accompany him to the shooting gallery and to drop the note behind the counter. He called me and told me to be in the shooting gallery at midnight. He and Slade may have seen each other in Bromberg's place. That made no difference, because they'd never met. Slade didn't know Drake, either. After Drake dropped the note, Barnaby waited until he fired at a target and he shot him. It was simple to step right out the door in the confusion. He'd called me first from a booth. He went to Violet's place, sold her on this wild story about the fake kidnapping or something similar. He got her to swear she'd say he had been there all evening. I doubt she connected Drake's death with the story Barnaby told her. He also got her to agree to deliver the brief case to me the following day, since Drake was dead and couldn't do it. He told her she'd have to be careful or she'd spoil the whole thing. That's why she disguised herself and hired Santa Claus to bring the package up.

"He also arranged for her to pick up the ransom the night after Christmas. He gave her two brief cases that Drake had bought for him. That's what seemed strange to Payne. He had seen Drake with two brief cases, exactly alike. He said it wasn't the *quality* that impressed him. It wasn't. It was the *quantity*.

"Barnaby had it timed so I would leave right at the end of the second scene. He wanted it that way for several reasons. One was that I would see him on stage and realize he couldn't possibly pick up the brief case from under my seat. That was his first entrance. If I'd left earlier he might have possibly been a suspect. Another thing was that he had to give Violet time to switch the brief cases. They didn't draw the curtain between scenes. They merely darkened the house a few seconds. Barnaby had figured a way to keep the house dark longer. He almost knocked the sets down when he made his entrance. He was holding up a set with his hand when the lights began to dim and he let it crash when the lights were out, so they'd have to keep the lights down until somebody righted the scenery or thought to pull the curtain.

"He'd realized I might plant somebody to watch my seat, so he had two brief cases ready. Violet had the empty one and she was standing right behind my seat with it when the lights went down. She had it concealed under that loose, sloppy-joe seater, probably. She switched the cases and when the lights came on, old Lennox saw the empty case and thought the one I'd left was still there. Tresca, the bearded sculptor, picked up the empty case and handed it to Violet and she gave it to Payne. She'd already got the one filled with money to Barnaby backstage.

"That's almost all of it. Barnaby thought I might come back downtown and he wanted to see what I would do, so he watched the theatre from that skid-row gin mill across the street. When he saw me go into the Weird Things shop, he peeped through the window a couple of times. When I left, he went in to see what Payne had told me. Probably the sight of Barnaby reminded Payne of the thing that he'd forgotten and he blurted it out. I suspect Drake had told him the brief cases were for Barnaby and when Barnaby found that out, he had to kill Payne. I think he

215

drove to New Haven after that. It would have been slow going because of the fog, for a way at least. He wouldn't have got there until this morning. When he did, he told Arlene off. He told her he had no intention of taking her away with him. She must have protested pretty violently. He gave her the black eye to convince her. There wasn't much to do. If she admitted the truth, she not only would lose her lover but her rich husband and any chance for a stage career as well and she might even be brought up as an accessory in extortion. Barnaby probably suggested she fake a hard case of amnesia. She took all identification from her bag. Barnaby gave her one of the ransom bills, for expenses to New York. He had left another bill beside Payne's body as a means of confusing the issue and maybe implicating Payne in the kidnapping plot.

"I don't think poor Violet is going to believe this second murder is a coincidence. She might have believed that about the first, but not two of them so close to home. So she's dangerous to Barnaby now. And people who are dangerous to Barnaby get killed."

Romano said, "It's a good story. I might buy it. Maybe I do. But the D.A. won't buy it. He likes proof."

"The ransom money will be the proof," Bart said.

"How do you plan to get that?" Romano asked.

"I'm going to buy it. It's too hot for Barnaby to hold. He'll sell it for half-price. That's why I borrowed twenty-five grand at six for five from Selig. That's why I want you to pose as Selig's strong boy when Barnaby gets back from Connecticut."

"He's already back," Romano answered mildly. "He's been back for about two hours."

"What?" roared Bart. "He can have killed that kid by now!"

"Uh-uh," Romano said. "We've had a stakeout at his place and one at the girl's place in case he went there. We had no proof, but he was a suspect and we wanted to talk to him. He's been in his place ever since he got back. And the girl hasn't left her house. At least that's the last report I had."

"Let's get down there, then," said Bart.

Romano tied his shoes. He took his new coat off the clothes tree, put it on and said, "Fits fine, don't it?" The lieutenant never wore a shoulder holster or other harness. He dropped a Police Positive into the pocket of the cashmere coat.

"You going to wear those new threads on a job like this?" Bart asked.

"Sure," Romano replied. "I'm supposed to be a hood. Hoods always dress up real nice. If I wore that old benny of mine, folks might think I was a cop."

sixteen

As the old Buick sped downtown Bart said to Romano, "Where has Barnaby been living since he broke up with Drake?"

"In a furnished room," Romano replied. "A furnished room in a private house on King Street. An Italian family owns the house."

They made numerous detours around one-way streets and finally entered King from Varick. It was an old street with trees and small brick houses. As they found a parking place, they saw the heavy-shouldered young detective Grierson walking toward a Ford sedan. Grierson was entering the sedan when Romano called to him. As they crossed the street, Romano said to Bart, "It was a two-man stakeout. I wonder why Richards isn't with him?"

When they reached the Ford Romano said to Grierson, "You all alone?"

Grierson nodded. "He came out alone a little while ago. He left his jalopy parked and started walking. We got out and followed him. It's hard to tail a walking man by car down here. Too many one-way streets. And you can't find a place to park."

"Is Richards on him?"

"Yeah. We tailed him to the house on Sullivan, the girl's house. There was a stakeout there, too, so there were four of us. We didn't need that many. I came back to get the car."

"He's in Violet Brent's house?" Hardin asked.

Grierson nodded.

"How long?" asked Bart. "How long has he been in there alone with her?"

"A little while," Grierson answered. "Half an hour or so, I guess."

Bart said to Romano, "Come on. We've got to get there if we're going to stop another murder."

The lieutenant said to Grierson, "You lead. We'll follow you in the Buick."

They piled into the car and drove to Sullivan Street. It took minutes, but to Hardin it seemed hours elapsed, that there were three stoplights on every corner. Richards was standing beside another car near the big brick house with the white trim. When Romano and Grierson went up to him, he said, "They left. Just after Grierson went to get the car. They're just around the corner now. Gaines and Ralls are on them. I came back to meet Grierson when he brought our car."

"Where did they go, man?" Hardin asked.

Richards looked at Bart doubtfully, turned to Romano and said, "Is he with you, Lieutenant?"

When Romano nodded, Richards said, "They went into that little theatre on Bleecker."

Bart and Romano walked fast toward Bleecker. One of

the detectives who had been staked out at Violet's place was lounging in front of the wino saloon where Hardin had met Old Fats the night before. The other was across the street, pretending to examine the photographs displayed in the small lobby of the theatre.

The man staked out in front of the saloon pretended to give Romano a light. He said, "They went up the alley and into the back part of the theatre through a stage door."

Romano and Hardin walked up the narrow alley to the stage door. The door was made of heavy metal and it was securely locked. The lieutenant hammered on it. Presently it was opened by Barnaby. The young actor wore tight-fitting blue jeans and a fleece-lined jacket. Hardin looked into the dim interior backstage. He did not see Violet Brent.

Barnaby said, "What is it? The theatre's closed today."

Bart said, "My name's Hardin. Hardin of the *Broadway Times*. I want to talk to you."

"What about?" asked Barnaby. He looked suspiciously at Romano.

Bart suddenly shoved the door open wider, throwing Barnaby slightly off balance. As he pushed by Barnaby, he said, "Come inside and I'll tell you."

Violet Brent suddenly appeared from a shadowy area. She looked pale and frightened. Her eyes seemed very large. She said to Barnaby, "This is the man who came to my place last night."

Romano walked into the theatre behind Hardin. He closed the heavy door after him. He stood glowering at

Barnaby and Hardin had to repress a grin at the spectacle of the lieutenant making like a menace.

"Send the girl away. What I've got to say is private," Hardin told Barnaby.

Barnaby's sulky, handsome face flushed with anger. He said, "What the hell is this? I don't like your attitude. . . ."

"Just send the girl away," Hardin interrupted.

Violet Brent's wide eyes stared at Hardin. She said, "No. I want to stay. I want to find out what this is all about. I'm tired of all these crazy stories. I want to know the truth."

Hardin didn't answer. His eyes held Barnaby. Barnaby stared back for a moment and Hardin thought of him as he had stood on the stage the night before with the scenery about to collapse around him, glaring at the audience, daring them to laugh.

Finally Barnaby shifted uncomfortably. He said to the girl, "You'd better go back to the office. Wait there for me. I want to hear what this man's got to say."

Violet hesitated. Hardin said, "Go on, honey. Go wait in the office."

She walked toward the stage, went down a few steps to the darkened theatre. She made her way up an aisle to the little office in the rear.

Barnaby said to Bart unpleasantly, "Now, mister. What's this all about?"

Bart said, "I've seen Arlene. She talked."

Barnaby glanced toward Romano. He said, "You aren't making much sense, you know. Who's this man?"

221

Bart said, "His name's Tony. He works for Moe Selig. You've heard of Selig, haven't you?"

Barnaby's face had become uncertain. Finally he said, "Selig? Selig's some kind of gangster, isn't he?"

"He prefers to call himself a businessman," Bart answered. "He wants to make a buy. That's why we've come here. To make a buy for Selig."

Barnaby grew angry again and the anger brought him assurance. He said, "All right, mister. I've had enough of this damned foolishness. I don't know what you're talking about. Say what you've got to say and get the hell out of here. Both of you."

"It's pretty simple," Bart explained. "Arlene and I were pretty good friends a long time ago. Before you came along. Before she married Slade. Maybe she never told you that, but she was my girl friend when she first came around Broadway. I talked to her in the hospital. She told me everything. Don't get nervous, though. It's all right. She hasn't told her husband or the cops."

Bart waited. Barnaby stared at him, said nothing.

Hardin said, "She'd like to make you squirm for the thing you did to her this morning. But she can't hurt you unless she hurts herself. You're big and you're ten years younger than I am, but I'm pretty sure I could take you if I wanted to." Bart chuckled. "Especially with my friend here to help out if things got tough. He's one of Selig's boys and he fights real dirty. But there's no pay-off in that. I don't give a damn about Arlene, not any more. I'm interested in money. So I went to Selig and told him I knew where fifty thousand bucks' worth of hot bills could be bought at a bargain price. I want to buy them."

"You're crazy, aren't you?" Barnaby said. He nodded, as if affirming it to himself. "That's what it is. You're just plain crazy."

Bart said, "The fifty grand is the hottest dough on earth right now, Howie boy. You've seen the papers. You know the serial numbers are plastered over all of them in big black type. Every police station in the country, every bank has got the numbers by now. You might possibly get by with breaking one or two of those hot twenties. But you won't break many, kid. One day you'll try to break one and they'll put the arm on you for kidnapping and murder. You might think you've got the murders licked. You haven't. Bromberg, the man who owns the shooting gallery, has got sharp eyes and a photographic memory. He can identify you as the man who chilled Drake when they stick you in the lineup. The old bum your girl used to deliver the brief case to me saw you last night going into Payne's place. He can put the finger on you, too. You might figure Arlene is so hot for you she'd come to your defense and say it wasn't really a kidnapping, even after what you did to her. She won't. She's what they call a woman scorned. She wouldn't turn you in, but she'd laugh out loud while they fry you in the hot squat, Howie."

Barnaby said again, "You're crazy. That's what it is, you're crazy." But he was wavering. His voice was more uncertain now.

Hardin grinned at him. He said, "You wouldn't stand

223

a chance, kid. You've got twenty-five hundred of those hot bills to pass. Somebody would spot one of them, just like they did with Hauptmann and all the other snatchers. Some bartender, maybe, or a little guy in dirty clothes who works in a gas station or an old lady who sits behind a cash register in a one-arm cafeteria. You couldn't pass the bills. You've got fifty thousand dollars' worth of nothing, Howie. But Selig can pass them. Selig helps to run a business enterprise they call the Syndicate. He could ship them out to books and numbers banks and gambling rooms all over the map. He could even get them spent in South America or Italy or Greece if he had to do it. That's why Selig wants to make a buy. You see that paper bag that Tony's got under his arm, Howie? There's twenty-five grand inside it. All in twenties. It's half of what you've stacked away, but there's a difference. You can spend the dough that's in that bag. It's not listed."

Howard Barnaby said, "It's crazy, but if you want to play, I'll play a little bit. So you think I've got the ransom money Slade paid for his wife. You say this Selig wants to buy it from me. If Selig wants to buy it, why are you here? What's in it for you, if Selig wants to buy?"

"Now we're getting somewhere, Howie," Bart declared. "Now you're talking sense. I'm here because I'm Selig's bird dog. I smelled the money out for him. And I get myself a nice fat slice when I take him back your bundle."

He turned to Romano, grinned and said, "Show him the dough, Tony. Make him drool a little."

There was a long, unpainted carpenter's table standing in the wings of the theatre. Romano walked to it. He turned the shopping bag upside-down and let the packages of currency spill over the table.

Bart said to Barnaby, "You can go a long, long way on that, kid. And you can travel first class, too. There's twelve hundred and fifty of those twenties and you won't get the arm put on you for spending a single one of them."

Barnaby walked slowly toward the table heaped with money. He walked stiff-legged, as if he were drawn there against his will. He picked up a couple of the packages of twenties, ran his thumb over the edges. He dropped the bills back to the table. He said to Bart, "The only trouble is I haven't got the ransom money."

Bart shrugged. "All right," he said. "If that's the way you want it, that's the way you get it. I gave you a chance to play ball and save the pieces. You don't want to play, so I'm going to holler copper. I'm going to Homicide and see a friend of mine named Romano. I'm going to tell him everything that Arlene told me. He's a tough cop, Howie. He'll make her talk to him and he'll make you talk, too, although he doesn't really have to, because he's got this Bromberg and the old bum to put the finger on you. I might as well get something out of this. If I can't get Selig's money, I'll get a little credit from my boss for solving his wife's kidnapping, anyway."

Hardin turned to Romano. "Pick up the money, Tony," he said. "This punk doesn't want it. We'll take it back to Selig."

Barnaby stared at Romano as he filled the paper bag with the currency. He shifted uncomfortably. He wet his lips with his tongue several times.

Bart started toward the stage door. He said, "So long, sucker. You might try running if you want to, but I'm laying six, two and even that Romano's got you in a back room before you get a chance to eat your dinner."

Barnaby said, "Wait. Wait a minute."

He walked out on the dimly lighted stage, peered through the gloom to make sure the door to the office that Violet Brent had entered was closed. He called softly to Bart, "Come out here."

Bart and Romano walked out on the stage where Erik Drake's sets depicted the town square of a mythical village in a desert. It was dimly lighted. Downstage right was a fountain. Bart remembered the waterless fountain from the Broadway production. In the final scene of the play, when Don Quixote makes a flourishing entrance and a defiant speech, the fountain spouts water for the first time in a thousand years.

The fountain that Drake had built was a large wooden tub, concealed in front by a pile of stones. The tub was filled with more stones that formed a mound from which the spray nozzle of a hose protruded. The hose led backstage to a water faucet.

Barnaby knelt down and began to remove stones from the wooden tub. When he had removed a few, he reached inside and brought forth the brief case that Hardin had left beneath the seat in the theatre. He said, "Give me the paper bag."

Bart nodded to Romano. Romano handed Barnaby the shopping bag. Barnaby looked inside it, hesitated. Then he handed the brief case over to Bart. He said, "A couple

226

of the twenties are missing. Selig shouldn't mind. He's getting it cheap enough."

Romano had a leather-cased badge in his hand now. He was extending it as he advanced on Barnaby. He said, "I'm a police officer. I'm arresting you."

Barnaby reacted fast.

He dropped to his knees behind the fountain, thrust his arm into the space from which he had removed the stones.

When his hand came out it held a gun and his finger had already begun to squeeze the trigger.

The gun did not explode.

Bart had seen no gun in Romano's hand, but Romano fired.

Barnaby slumped to the stage.

The actor's final scene was not a pretty one. As Bart knelt beside him, Barnaby's breath wheezed out and it sounded like a wistful sigh. Presently blood began to flow steadily from his open mouth.

A door slammed open in the back of the theatre.

A girl was screaming.

The girl was running down the darkened aisle, calling "Howard! Howard!"

As she stumbled up the short flight of steps to the stage, Bart grabbed her, shielded her from seeing the dead man behind the fountain. He said, "Don't look, Violet. He's dead. There's nothing you can do. He tried to kill a police officer."

The girl sobbed, her head against Bart's chest. Then she

227

looked up at him. "He said it was a joke. A publicity stunt. He said it was a joke, and now he's dead."

Bart said, "It wasn't any joke. He killed two men."

"I know," she sobbed. "Today I was almost sure that he was lying, that he'd been lying all the time. I—I loved him. He got me into it. He told me it was a joke, a kind of stunt that would get him publicity. He said you were in on it and you double-crossed him and kept the money. He said you killed Drake and Payne because they knew you had double-crossed him and stolen the money."

"Go back to the office, Violet. Go back there and wait," Bart said. "We'll come back to you in just a minute."

The girl walked back through the darkness.

Romano was sitting in a chair beside a glass-topped table on the terrace of the hotel set. His head hung down between his shoulders as if he were very ill. His swarthy face had paled and beads of sweat oozed over it.

Bart went to him, said, "Are you all right?"

Romano nodded. "Did you see the look in his eyes?" he asked. "I knew he was going to kill. You've been a cop as long as I have, you get to know that look. It always means they're going to kill. You have to shoot first when you see their eyes like that. I had to do it."

Bart said, "Yes. You had to do it."

Romano raised his head. "I had to do it," he repeated, "but that doesn't help. It always makes me sick. I've had to kill like that before and it's always made me sick. A man with a nervous stomach should never be a cop."

He looked down at his coat. There was a singed, blackened hole in it. Romano said, "The gun was in my over-coat. When I tried to take it out it caught on the pocket flap. I had to shoot him through the pocket. Cops shouldn't have flaps on their pockets. My wife and kid are going to give me hell. I've ruined the brand new coat they gave me for a Christmas present."

seventeen

It was nearly nine o'clock at night when Hardin reached Slade's place on Gracie Square.

Hodgson's face was blank as ever when he took Bart's coat and hat. But Bart thought there was a smirk behind the blandness, a servant's secret gloating over the scandal of his employer's wife.

Slade was waiting in the study this time, in the warm room with its deep leather chairs and its bright sporting prints and its amusing Cobbett oils of the London prize ring.

Slade sat slumped. The high color had faded from his face and his usually immaculate linen was rumpled and sweated at the collar line. The eyes beneath his bushy black brows were red-filamented and slightly dazed. On the table beside his chair a brandy bottle was half-empty. Bart had never seen Slade intoxicated. He noted that even now he drank from the proper glass. A large balloon inhaler was in his hand. The hand was trembling slightly.

Bart said, "Did Romano call you?"

Slade said, "Yes. He called. He told me everything. I owe you an apology. I was sure you were mixed up in it."

"I didn't come for apologies," Bart told him. "I came to get the check you promised me, the reward. The police have your money. There may be a couple of twenties missing. One was in your wife's purse. Another was found beside Payne's body. The Public Administrator will turn that over to you in time, I guess."

Slade said, "The money never mattered. I've made out your check."

He picked up a blue-tinted check on the Brokers Bank, handed it to Bart. Bart examined it briefly. He folded it, put it in his empty wallet.

Bart said, "I guess that ends all the business there is between us. I've told Pops Taylor he's managing editor until you find a replacement for me. Pops won't take the job for good. He thinks that he's too old and he wants to stick to his horses till he dies. But there's one favor I'd like to ask. Maybe I can do you a favor in return."

Slade looked up and said, "Name it."

"I'll name the favor I can do you first," Bart said. "It's presumptuous, but it may be helpful. I suggest you let this kidnap story die a natural death, just give it out that she was kidnapped by Barnaby and that the brutal experience has given her a nervous breakdown. You can say she's left for a sanitarium in Europe. While she's abroad, she can get her divorce in Paris. That way the scandal of her running away, trying to extort money from you, won't hit the papers. Romano is willing to co-operate. So is Broderick, I understand."

Slade looked at Bart. "Your advice is no good to me," he said. "I'm not sending her away. I want her, no matter

231

what she's done. I always buy whatever I want. I always pay for it. Usually I pay for it with money. This time I'll pay with pride."

Slade drank from the inhaler. "Now," he said. "What was the favor you had to ask from me?"

"It was about the girl," said Bart. "The kid named Violet Brent. She was in it, but she didn't know what she was doing. She's not guilty of anything except being foolishly in love and believing an impossible story. Romano won't press charges against her unless you insist. I wanted to ask you to forget about her."

Slade looked up at Hardin and the vacant expression faded slowly from his eyes. It was replaced by a look of speculative shrewdness. He said, "I'll make a deal. I'll forget about the girl if you won't quit me on the *Broadway Times.*"

Bart looked puzzled. He said, "Why should you want me? There are plenty of men around can work the job."

"There aren't many who can take it," Slade replied. "The Street gets them all in time. Most of them anyway. They take to dope or drink or maybe it's just women who get them down. But it's hard to find a man who can walk The Street and keep his balance. You can."

"If you can swallow so much pride, I can swallow a little bit, I guess," Bart answered. "Besides I've got nothing to go holy about. I mistrusted you as much as you mistrusted me. I thought you'd killed your wife. I'll stay. I'll be at work tomorrow."

Slade said, "It's a deal. I'll forget the girl."

Bart picked up the paper shopping bag that was stuffed

with Selig's money. He started for the door. Then he turned and said, "I want to tell you about the reward. It's not for me. It's interest I have to pay to Selig for lending me that twenty-five grand I used as bait for Barnaby."

"You deserve a reward for what you've done, I guess," Slade admitted. "But I'm not giving it to you. Not in a lump sum, anyway. If I did, you'd bet it all on a card tonight or a horse tomorrow. You're a gambler. When a millionaire bets a hundred thousand on a horse, he's not a gambler. He can afford to lose. It's the man who bets every cent he's got who is a gambler, no matter how little it is. You're that kind of gambler, Hardin."

Bart said, "It's no fun winning unless it hurts to lose."

"In most ways we're about as different as men can get," Slade went on. "But in one way we're alike. We play it our way or we don't play at all. And neither one of us is going to change. I'll do something for you, but I'll do it my way. I'll raise your salary fifty dollars a week. If you hang around long enough, you'll get your five thousand —in dribbles."

Bart said, "That's fine. I'll use the extra dough to employ a secretary. Your business office is too tight to hire me one."

Slade tried to end it on a feeble jest. He said, "It will be interesting to note if she's blonde, brunette, or titian. You've always played the field."

"You can't hire a glamor girl for fifty bucks a week," Bart told him. "Not nowadays. My secretary will be an old man over seventy. His name is James Lennox and he was a fine actor once. I doubt that he knows shorthand,

233

but it will be worth the money just to look at an honest man occasionally."

Bart retrieved his coat and hat from Hodgson. He walked to East End Avenue and found a cab. He told the driver to take him to Madison Square Garden.

When they pulled up in front of the Garden Bart searched his pockets. He found two one-dollar bills. He handed them to the driver and said, "Keep it." Then he said, "Wait a minute." He found thirty-six cents in change and handed that to the driver, too. "You might as well have this," he said.

There was an ice show in the Garden, but the crowd had streamed in long before. There was a lonely sentinel outside the spacious lobby of the big arena. It was old Tom Trigg, the Negro heavy who had met them all and whipped a lot of them.

Bart said, "I'm glad to see you didn't hock my old man's coat."

The Negro grinned. "Wouldn't hock it, Mist' Bart," he said. "Like this coat better'n hot biscuits soaked in beef-steak juice. When I wear this coat and brace a mark, it ain't bumming. It's a legitimate transaction."

"You always get the rumble if a game is on," said Bart. "I've got to see Moe Selig. Is he in a game somewhere?"

"Man, I'll say!" old Tom exclaimed. "But it ain't a game for you to get in. It's a real high-roller, this one, and it's private. Couple of big Syndicate torpedoes from St. Louis just came to town. Seems out in Saint Loo all they crave is craps, so Mist' Moe is obliging them. Mist' Lenny Fassio hisself is in this one. It's just around the corner in that old warehouse Mist' Lenny owns."

"I know it," Bart said. "The one near Ninth. I hear they stored bootleg booze there during Prohibition."

Old Tom cackled. "Man," he said, "they stored so much hot stuff there one time or the other it's a wonder that place ain't exploded long ago."

Bart turned up Fiftieth and walked toward Ninth. There had been floating crap games in this warehouse before and he had been a shooter. He turned up a dark alley that ran beside the building. He found a bell high up in the framework of the steel door.

The door slid open and one of Selig's dead-eyed goons peered out at Bart.

Bart said, "Tell Selig Hardin wants to see him."

The lookout said, "He's busy."

Bart pushed through the door. "Tell Selig I've got a great big bag of money for him," he said.

The goon looked doubtful for a moment. Then he bolted the door and walked away.

Presently Selig came down a flight of stairs. Hardin handed him the shopping bag. "Here it is, bag and all," he said. "It's the same dough that you gave me. You can count it."

Selig said, "I don't have to count it, chum. If it wasn't what you say it is, you wouldn't be here. I was a little worried when I heard the Law had put the arm on you. Worried about the dough, I mean."

Bart took out his wallet, handed Selig the blue check on the Brokers Bank. "It's signed by Maddox Slade," he said. "Is that okay?"

Selig looked at the check and said, "Kosher." Then he began to laugh. "That Lenny Fassio!" he exclaimed. "He's blowing his top because he's been throwing snake-eyes and boxcars all night. Just wait till he hears this. He flipped his wig when I told him I'd let you make this borrow. He said he wouldn't take it as organization business, that a guy like you wasn't good for dough like that. He said I was making the loan personally to you. So now I take the interest. Let's see, you made the borrow around four and it's a little after nine. That's a thousand an hour interest. Man, will Lenny burn!"

When Selig had had his laugh he said, "I told him. I said I lent dough to this guy's old man and he always paid. I lent dough to this guy himself many's the time, I said, and he always paid before his time was up. His credit's good with Selig, I told that to Lenny."

Bart said, "I'm glad my credit's good. I want to make another borrow."

Selig looked at Bart with amazement for a minute and then he exploded with laughter again. Tears ran down his cheeks and he bent over and slapped his thighs.

"Man," he said, "you're a character! A real gone hipster, that's what you are. You pay me back twenty-five gees with five grand interest and you want to make another borrow. How much is it this time?"

"Five bucks," Hardin answered. "I'm hungry and I haven't got the price of dinner."